D0284288

Coy Library of Shippensburg
73 West King Street
Shippensburg PA 17257

THE UNDERCOVER
BOOK
LIST

by

COLLEEN NELSON

pajamapress
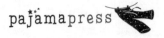

First published in Canada and the United States in 2021

Text copyright © 2021 Colleen Nelson
This edition copyright © 2021 Pajama Press Inc.
This is a first edition.
10 9 8 7 6 5 4 3 2 1

All rights reserved. No part of this publication may be reproduced, stored in a retrieval system or transmitted, in any form or by any means, without the prior written consent of the publisher or a licence from The Canadian Copyright Licensing Agency (Access Copyright). For an Access Copyright licence, visit www.accesscopyright.ca or call toll free 1.800.893.5777.

www.pajamapress.ca   info@pajamapress.ca

The publisher gratefully acknowledges the support of the Canada Council for the Arts and the Ontario Arts Council for its publishing program. We acknowledge the financial support of the Government of Canada through the Canada Book Fund (CBF) for our publishing activities.

Library and Archives Canada Cataloguing in Publication

Title: The undercover book list / by Colleen Nelson.
Names: Nelson, Colleen, author.
Description: First edition.
Identifiers: Canadiana 20210177047 | ISBN 9781772781878 (hardcover)
Classification: LCC PS8627.E555 U53 2021 | DDC jC813/.6—dc23

Publisher Cataloging-in-Publication Data (U.S.)

Names: Nelson, Colleen, author.
Title: The Undercover Book List / by Colleen Nelson.
Description: Toronto, Ontario Canada : Pajama Press, 2021. | Summary: "An anonymous correspondence between two seventh graders becomes an unlikely friendship after they start leaving notes in a school library book. Bookish Jane MacDonald is seeking a new friend after her best friend Sienna moves away; reputed troublemaker Tyson Flamand stumbles upon the first note while waiting for a detention. Both end up in a race to improve Tyson's grades—and their teachers' understanding of him—so that he can help complete the school team for Jane's cherished Kid Lit Quiz competition and win a trip to the championship in Sienna's new city"— Provided by publisher.
Identifiers: ISBN 978-1-77278-187-8 (hardcover)
Subjects: LCSH: Identity (Psychology) in adolescence – Juvenile fiction. | School libraries -- Juvenile fiction. | Helping behavior – Juvenile fiction. | BISAC: JUVENILE FICTION / Social Themes / Friendship. | JUVENILE FICTION / Social Themes / Self-Esteem & Self-Reliance. | JUVENILE FICTION / School & Education.
Classification: LCC PZ7.1N457Un |DDC 813.6 – dc23

Cover illustration—Scot Ritchie
Cover and book design—Lorena González Guillén

Manufactured by Friesens
Printed in Canada

Pajama Press Inc.
469 Richmond St. E, Toronto, ON M5A 1R1

Distributed in Canada by UTP Distribution
5201 Dufferin Street Toronto, Ontario Canada, M3H 5T8

Distributed in the U.S. by Ingram Publisher Services
1 Ingram Blvd. La Vergne, TN 37086, USA

For Gail Winskill

CHAPTER 1

Jane

I didn't want to be late. Not today. But my six-year-old sister, Kate, had been extra picky about the way I braided her hair and then she'd stopped to play with our neighbor's dog. By the time I dropped her off at the primary entrance and raced around to the middle school doors of Forest Hills School the bell was about to ring.

"Sorry," I apologized as soon as I found Sienna. Before I could say anything else, Sienna pulled a small, shiny box out of her jacket pocket.

"I got you something," Sienna said. "I was going to give it to you at the end of the day, but I can't wait."

She passed it to me and I lifted the lid. Inside was

a necklace with a silver heart pendant. *Best Friend* was engraved on it. "I love it," I whispered. "Thank you."

"Even if I'm not here, we're still besties." We'd said that to each other so many times since we found out she was moving, I'd lost count.

I'd promised her I wouldn't cry, but tears sprang to my eyes at her words. By tomorrow, Sienna would be on a plane to her new home too far away.

"I have something for you too," I said. Kate wasn't the only thing that had slowed me down this morning. Sienna's gift weighed a ton.

I unzipped my backpack and pulled out her present. The illustrated hardcover edition of *Harry Potter and the Sorcerer's Stone*. Sienna had wanted it for ages. "You can read it and think of me." She clutched it to her chest, speechless.

The bell for homeroom rang and neither of us moved. A wave of emptiness rolled over me even though Sienna was standing right there. I swallowed the lump in my throat and took a deep breath. I needed to be strong for Sienna. As hard as it was to say goodbye to my best friend, it was worse for her. Moving to a new city, starting over at a new school, making new friends…at least I'd still be in familiar surroundings.

"I'm going to miss you so much," she said.

"We can call and text," I said, trying to stay upbeat. "And FaceTime! You'll be so busy making new friends, you'll barely have time to miss me."

She snorted with disbelief. "Yeah, right."

"Here, help me with my necklace," I said, changing the subject. I lifted my hair so she could attach the clasp, then turned to face her. The heart dangled just below the hollow of my throat. "How does it look?"

"Perfect," Sienna said.

Today was going to be sad. But tomorrow would be worse. I couldn't imagine coming to school and not seeing her. The first half of seventh grade had been tough—and not just because I'd known my best friend was moving. During the summer, my dad had been posted overseas as the Chief of Staff for a peacekeeping mission in the Middle East. It wasn't the first time he'd had to leave us because of his job in the military, but this was the farthest he'd gone and for the longest time. Sienna had made it bearable with sleepovers and movie marathons. For my birthday, because she knew I loved mysteries, she'd even planned a scavenger hunt. It took us all day to follow the clues. She'd made my twelfth birthday one I'd always remember.

Today, it was my turn to repay the favor. I wanted to

make this the best last day ever. The second bell rang. "Come on. We should get to homeroom," I said.

Just like I'd planned, Aisha was on the look-out and as soon as she spotted us coming down the hallway, she darted into Mr. Lee's room. I paused just before we got to the door and let Sienna open it.

Thirty voices shouted, "Surprise!" Maybe it was seeing everyone cheering for her, or the huge banner that hung across the back window that read *We'll Miss You, Sienna*, but Sienna froze in the doorway and then burst into tears.

"That was the best worst day I've ever had." Sienna sighed, summing up my feelings exactly. It was the end of the day and her backpack bulged with goodbye cards. We were waiting for her mom at the front of the school. As soon as I said my final goodbye, I'd walk to the primary doors to pick up Kate.

"This time tomorrow, you'll be in your new house," I said.

Sienna nodded but couldn't have looked less excited.

"I hope you can come for a visit."

"Me too," I said, even though Mom had told me it wasn't in the budget, at least not this year.

A familiar car pulled up to the curb. Sienna's mom, Cindy, got out to give me a hug goodbye. "Sienna's so lucky to have a friend like you," she said. Her eyes were misty too. *Why are you moving if it's making everyone so sad?* I wanted to ask. Sienna threw herself at me for a final squeeze. "I left you a surprise. It's in the library," she whispered.

"What is it?"

"I can't tell you. Your clue is that it's *safer approved.*"

Safer approved? She gave me a mysterious look and opened the car door. Cindy walked around to her side and got in. "Let me know when you figure it out!" Sienna said. She slid into the passenger seat and rolled down the window. "I'll text you when I get there!" she called as Cindy pulled into traffic.

I stared after the taillights until the car turned a corner. A couple of primary kids walked past. Kate would be waiting. As I walked around the school, I repeated the clue she'd given me. *Safer approved.* Only Sienna could have found a way to make me look forward to coming to school tomorrow.

CHAPTER 2

Tyson

Tyson had spent that morning staring at his principal's receding hairline—there was more of his dark-skinned forehead than there used to be—and listening to a lecture. Another prank had gone too far. But it *had* got him out of a science quiz he hadn't studied for, which had been the whole point. Mr. Morangi's words echoed in Tyson's head as he walked home. "You need to make better choices…not everything's a joke…take things seriously."

The truth was that school felt like a too-tight shirt that pinched under his arms and choked him around the neck. Joking around with his friends made it bearable. He never meant to hurt anyone but sometimes that's what happened. Like today with Connor's jersey. A total accident! Too bad Mr. Morangi didn't think so.

When he got home, there was a note on the fridge. It was right below his younger sister Ava's Honor Roll certificate and his older brother Max's high school Athlete of Month Award. *Tyson: Put lasagna in oven at 350 for an hour and a half.* As usual, he was the only one home. Ava had dance, Max had hockey, and his parents were at work.

He turned the oven on, poured some juice, and grabbed a snack. The oven took forever to heat up. He'd come back in a few minutes and put the dinner in.

When Tyson got to his room, he kicked the door shut behind him and flopped into the purple armchair he'd dragged up from the basement. His parents wouldn't buy him a real gaming chair, so he made do with this one, even though it smelled like mildew and creaked when he sat on it. Tyson plugged his headphones into his Xbox and turned the power on.

The title sequence for *Mutant-Z* flashed across the screen. It was about a group of mutants who wanted to take over Earth. They battled humans for control of key sites. Players could either be a mutant or a human. Tyson was always on the side of the mutants. He'd created a character named Lizardo who could spin his head almost 360 degrees and crawl like a lizard up buildings and across ceilings. The mutants didn't get weapons, but they could steal them from the humans. Tyson recognized a player and asked to join his mutant army.

As Lizardo dropped into the game Tyson was able to forget about his day at school; the reading response he hadn't finished and the quiz he'd failed. He wished, as he often did, that he lived in the *Mutant-Z* world, and not this one.

CHAPTER 3

Jane

As usual, Grandpa was waiting for us when we got home. Even though I was old enough to look after Kate, Grandpa insisted on coming by. Which was fine with me. I loved seeing him every day.

"Hi, Grandpa," I called. I dumped my backpack and jacket at the door and kicked off my shoes.

"In here." He always sat in the living room, watching for us out the front window. Grandpa looked like the man from the Monopoly game, minus the top hat and dollar bills bursting out of his pocket. He had the same pinky-hued skin tone and ring of white hair on his otherwise bald head. His eyes crinkled when he smiled, which was a lot.

"How'd it go?" he asked when I plopped beside him on the couch. He meant the party, but he also knew how much I'd been dreading Sienna's last day.

"She was totally surprised, but it was—" I broke off. "Sad." Kate curled up on the other side of him.

"You know," Grandpa said, "your mom had a best friend who went to a different school when they started junior high. She said she'd never make another friend like that girl."

"But she did, right?"

"Not really."

"Thanks, Grandpa," I said sarcastically.

"I'm kidding!" His eyes twinkled behind his glasses. "Of course she did! It took some time. Replacing a friend like Sienna won't be easy, but it will happen." His mustache quivered with a smile.

Sienna and I had found each other three years ago on her first day at Forest Hills School. We were in the library and I was returning the book she was about to request. Just like that, we had an instant friendship. Mrs. Chin, the librarian, called it a match made in heaven.

Sienna loved reading as much as I did. Last year when we were old enough to enter the Kid Lit Quiz, we had that in common too. Our teacher, Ms. Krauss, who coached the quiz team, said she'd never had two kids who read as much as we did.

"How about a snack?" Grandpa asked. "Grandma baked a pie. We're supposed to save it for dessert, but…" He wiggled his eyebrows. "I won't tell if you won't tell."

Grandma thought most problems could be fixed with food. According to her there was no situation dessert couldn't make better.

As Grandpa took out the plates and Kate got the forks, I pulled the tinfoil off an apple pie that made my mouth water. "How about some ice cream?" Grandpa asked, going to the freezer. He put the carton on the counter and got out the special ice cream spoon. "One scoop, or two?" he asked.

"Two!" Kate and I both said. As Grandpa dug into the ice cream, his hand started to tremble. The tremble turned into a shake and he dropped the spoon. It fell on the counter with a loud clatter.

"Grandpa?"

He looked at me, embarrassed. "My arm got a little weak."

"Here, let me." I picked up the spoon and dropped two scoops on top of each piece of pie.

Grandpa kept staring straight ahead. His mustache was quivering again, but not in a good way.

CHAPTER 4

Tyson

In the game, Lizardo was chasing a human who had evaded him for the last hour and a half.

He was searching an abandoned warehouse for his prey. His lizard feet clicked across the brick walls, the only giveaway to his opponent. He heard the other character breathing and saw a flash of movement on his right. With a start, he realized it was a trap! He'd been led to the warehouse to be ambushed by a team of humans!

He had to get out of the warehouse. In his bedroom, Tyson leaned forward in his chair, his body tensed. If he could create a diversion, he might have a chance to escape through a window. He had one smoke canister that he'd stolen from another player, and now was the time to use it. A thick vapor filled the air when he tossed it on the ground. Lizardo leapt and grabbed onto a rafter, swinging himself up.

Below him, two humans had heat-seeking goggles and breathing apparatuses. Laser lights on their guns moved erratically through the smoke. If he could crawl to the window without being spotted, he'd be safe.

He was so close to freedom he could taste it. But then: "Mutant!" A human spotted him and started firing. Bullets whizzed past him. The window was close. His lizard claws moved expertly across the narrow rafter. He was almost there. He was going to make it!

"Tyson!"

The screen went black.

His mom stood in front of him holding the cable, which was no longer attached to the outlet. He stared at her in shock.

"The lasagna," his mom said. "You forgot to put it in the oven."

She was waiting for him to say something, but he had no words. He stared at the screen. He'd been so close!

"Honestly, Ty! How hard is it to do one thing?"

"I meant to put it in. I just forgot."

"Because you were playing that game," she said, shaking her head, exasperated. "Mr. Morangi called. Again."

"Connor doesn't know how to take a joke."

"You ruined his jersey!"

He held her gaze. "Not on purpose. And it's not ruined. It just needs to be washed."

"I told Mr. Morangi it wouldn't happen again." She shot him a final warning look as she dropped the cable and left the room.

Tyson felt bad about dinner, but worse about the game. The other players would have seen Lizardo plummet to his death and think he'd been shot by the humans. But really, he'd died because his mom had unplugged the game. *I'm going to beat this level. I'll play all night if I have to.*

CHAPTER 5

Jane

Grandpa put Kate to bed and hung around until Mom got home. Mom is a scientist who specializes in vaccine research. This week was a big deal for her because the CEO and president of her company was visiting. She had to give a presentation on her research and wanted it to be perfect. "Tell me everything," she said after Grandpa had gone. "Was Sienna surprised? Did she like her gift?"

I nodded. "She gave me this." Mom leaned in to get a better look at the necklace. "She also said there was a surprise in the library for me and that it was *safer approved*, whatever that means."

Mom raised her eyebrows. "Intriguing." My love of a good mystery was no secret.

"I'm going to get started on it first thing tomorrow."
Knowing I had a mystery to solve took some of the
sting out of Sienna's departure. "She's going to text me
as soon as she gets to her new house." Sienna had shown
me the real estate agent's video. The house had an ocean
view and was on the kind of cul-de-sac that was made
for riding bikes and setting up lemonade stands. I bet
they had neighborhood barbecues too.

"I wish I could go out there." I sighed.

Mom gave me a sympathetic look. "I know you
do, but things are just too up in the air." She meant
because Dad was away—at least, I thought that was
what she meant. Sienna was the second person I'd
had to say goodbye to in the last six months. At least
Dad's posting was only for a year. Sienna's move was
for forever.

I stifled a yawn, but Mom caught it. "You should get
to sleep," she said. "You've got that mystery to solve."

Ordinarily, I'd have fought to stay up for a while
longer, but she was right. Good detectives needed to be
sharp. If there was one thing I'd learned about Sienna
when she created my birthday scavenger hunt, it was that
she loved leaving clues as much as I loved finding them.

CHAPTER 6

Tyson

"Mom says you have to wake up!" Ava stuck her head into his room and turned on the light. She looked a lot like Tyson. Brown hair, hazel eyes, a few freckles across her white-skinned cheeks and nose.

"Go away!" Tyson said, burying his face in his pillow. His shoulders ached and his fingers were stiff from playing *Mutant-Z* until past midnight. Way past midnight.

"It's 8:15!" Ava said. "You're gonna be late."

"I don't care."

Ava's swat woke him up again. "Get up! Mom's already in a bad mood. You're just going to make it worse for all of us."

"Is he awake?" Tyson's mom bellowed from down the hall.

"Yeah!" Ava shouted, shoving Tyson's shoulder so he rolled onto his back.

His mom opened the door to his room. "I thought you said he was awake."

Ava sighed and got to her feet. "He's awake, just not upright."

Tyson's mom marched over to his bed and ripped the covers off him. "Tyson Edward! I've had it! What time did you go to bed last night?"

Tyson kept quiet. She wouldn't like the answer.

"It's that game," she said. She spun around and marched to the low table that held his TV and Xbox. For the second time in two days, she yanked the cable out of the wall and picked up the small, shiny black console and held it in her hands. "You were playing on this thing all night and now you're too tired to wake up." She shook her head. "I warned you that you'd lose it if this kept happening. You'll get your game back *if* you can make it through the rest of the week without any phone calls from the school. *And* if you wake up on time every morning."

Tyson's mom didn't wait for him to say anything. She turned on her heel and left the room. The console cable dragged on the floor behind her.

Tyson stared after his mom, shocked. He didn't know how he'd get through the week without playing *Mutant-Z*. Lizardo might have only been a video game character, but he felt like a real friend to Tyson.

What was he going to do without him?

CHAPTER 7

Jane

When I got to school, the first place I went was the library. "Sienna said she left a surprise here for me," I told Mrs. Chin. "Do you know anything about it?"

Mrs. Chin shook her head.

"She said it was *safer approved*."

Mrs. Chin frowned, repeating the words under her breath. "I have no idea. But go ahead and look around."

Where to start? Nothing in the library seemed out of the ordinary, but I still wasn't sure what I was looking for.

My determination to solve the mystery by the time Sienna texted from her new house started to fizzle.

With no other clues to go on, I already felt like I was at a dead end. The first bell rang, and I reluctantly left the library and went to homeroom. But when I got there, I paused in the doorway. Mr. Lee was glaring at Tyson Flamand. "Did you really throw Connor's Timberwolves hat on the roof?"

Connor's arms were crossed over his chest. He liked the Minnesota Timberwolves and was constantly teased for it by Tyson and his friends. It didn't matter that Connor was the best basketball player in the class, or that he'd made the school's elite team. Yesterday, Tyson, Andrew, and Affan had taken his Timberwolves jersey and hidden it—in the trash can! That had got all three of them in trouble, especially when the jersey was pulled out covered in strawberry yogurt.

"The wind took it," Tyson said, sniggering.

Connor fumed. "You stole it off my head!" Anything that ended up on the roof of the school had to be rescued by the school's custodian who had a hundred more urgent jobs. Connor would be waiting a while to get his hat back.

Mr. Lee stretched his arm out like a traffic cop and pointed to the door. "Go to the office. You can sort it out with Mr. Morangi." Mr. Lee rarely sent kids to the office. He must have been really fed up with Tyson.

"I'm sorry. It was a joke!"

But Mr. Lee didn't change his mind.

Tyson left, shaking his head, as Aisha arrived. "What was that all about?" she asked me.

"Tyson threw Connor's hat on the roof and Mr. Lee sent him to the office."

"Tyson's funny, but sometimes he takes things too far." I nodded and both of us went to our seats.

"Let's get started," Mr. Lee said when everyone was settled. He stood at the front of the class with a stack of index cards. "It's the first of April. Time to add to our Other Words for Me board."

We'd started the Other Words for Me board on the first day of school in September. It was a year-long project. At the beginning of each month, we picked a word that reflected how we were feeling right then. It could be a wish, an emotion, or a goal, but it could only be one word.

"Think about what you're looking forward to, or if you've changed over the last month. Maybe you're more confident or feeling more relaxed about school." He caught Lingbin's eye. Lingbin had only been living here for a month and had written *anxious*, in English and Mandarin on his last card. "Or maybe you have something to celebrate." This time he looked at Mitchell, who'd just had his Bar Mitzvah.

"When you've chosen your word, write it on one side and a short explanation on the back. Then bring it to me and I'll staple it to the bulletin board." There was rustling and some quiet chatter as people got out their pencil cases, or talked about different words they might choose.

My word for last month had been *waiting*. I was waiting for Dad to come home, and also for the date of the Kid Lit Quiz regional tournament to be set. And of course, it was the final month before Sienna moved.

Beside my word, Sienna had stapled hers: *change*. Reading it now gave me a twinge of missing her.

Minju Park had chosen *vivacious*. With her energy and easy laugh, I thought of her as a firecracker. She was the star of the basketball team and friendly with everyone. Connor's word was *teamwork*. His basketball team was having a great season. Andrew had also tried out for the elite team. He'd made it to the last round before getting cut. His word was *taller*. He was about the same size as me and was convinced that if he grew, it would improve his chances next year. His best friend, Affan, had written *motivated*. It sounded like his family put a lot of pressure on him to do as well as his older brother, who had a scholarship to McGill.

Marcus had just come back from a month-long vacation in the Philippines to visit his family. His word last month had been *palaam* which is goodbye in Tagalog. My friend Rafaella had written *stylish* on hers. She kept offering to give the rest of us fashion makeovers, but I was perfectly comfortable in jeans and a hoodie. Aisha, who now wore a head scarf, had picked *bold*. It was the perfect word for her. She wasn't afraid to speak her mind and I was sure she'd run the country one day. Stella had drawn a manga version of herself dreaming of the word *thoughtful*. Tyson's word last month had been *word*, which was no better than the word from the month before: *goal*. Mr. Lee *had* said to write a word or a goal…he just didn't expect anyone to take it literally. Like with a lot of his assignments, Tyson hadn't taken Other Words for Me seriously.

Mr. Lee passed out the index cards and asked, "What will your April word be?" With Sienna gone, only one word could sum up how I was feeling.

Lonely.

But that was so sad. I didn't want *lonely* to haunt me for the rest of the year on the bulletin board. Even if it was true right now. Sienna wouldn't want me moping around missing her. That was why she'd left the clue in the library. Just thinking about solving it raised my spirits and gave me something to look forward to.

I wrote my word on the card and brought it to Mr. Lee. "*Hopeful*," Mr. Lee said.

It summed up my feelings for me and for Sienna. I wanted her to be happy at her new school. "Good choice," he said.

We went to Ms. Gill's class for second period math. Half my brain was listening to Ms. Gill's lesson on balancing equations, and the other half was considering Sienna's clue. It must have something to do with a book, but which one? And what did *safer approved* mean?

"Jane? Do you know the answer?" Ms. Gill's voice ripped through my thoughts. Her many bangles jangled on her arm and the small diamond stud in her nose glinted against her skin. On the first day of school, she'd worn a bright pink sari. It was the most beautiful outfit I'd ever seen.

"Uh." I stared at her, blinking stupidly. I had no idea what the question was.

But Ms. Gill wasn't one of those teachers who liked to catch kids out. She smiled at me and pointed to the question on the board: $8 \times 9 = 65 + X$. "Can you solve for X?"

"X is 7," I said. "Both sides equal 72."

"Excellent!" Ms. Gill beamed at me. "Solving for X isn't hard when you know what clues to look for."

I wrote down the equation in my notebook. My pen hovered over the X. Something about that letter felt familiar. One of my favorite books had a character named Mr. X. In the back of my mind, something clicked. Sienna hadn't meant *safer*, she'd meant *Safer*, with a capital *S*! Safer was the main character in *Liar & Spy* by Rebecca Stead. In the story, Safer and Georges (the *s* is silent) follow Mr. X, a suspected spy who lives in their building.

Of course Sienna would pick that book as a clue! She knew how much I loved mysteries. I sat through math impatiently, waiting for a chance to get to the library at morning break to see if my hunch was right.

CHAPTER 8

Tyson

Normally Tyson didn't worry about getting sent to the office. But today, his mom's words about holding his Xbox hostage echoed in his mind.

"Have a seat, Ty," Mrs. Hardy said when he got to the office. While he sat there, Mr. Lee buzzed the office. Tyson caught snippets of his tinny-sounding voice through the intercom. "…threw Connor's hat… roof…read…finish a book…Friday."

"Okay, I'll let him know." Mrs. Hardy turned to Tyson. "Mr. Morangi is busy for a while. Do you want to get a book?"

He shook his head at Mrs. Hardy. She raised her eyebrows and gave him a silent, *Are you sure?* face.

He was sure. He hated reading. He'd rather just sit in the office chair.

Tyson had been waiting for fifteen minutes when Mr. Morangi came out of his office. "I'm late for a meeting," he told Mrs. Hardy. When Mr. Morangi noticed Tyson he arched an eyebrow at him. "What are you doing here?"

"I *accidentally* threw a hat on the roof."

"Whose hat was it?" Mr. Morangi asked.

Thinking about Connor trying to get the hat back made Tyson want to grin. Snatching it off his head and racing away with it had been funny. But Connor was fast and just before he tackled Tyson, Tyson had tossed the hat in the air, expecting to catch it again. Instead, the wind took it.

"Connor's. But technically, it was the wind, not me, that made it land on the roof."

Mr. Morangi frowned. "Yesterday we talked about making good choices and what would happen if you didn't." Mr. Morangi looked at his watch. "I think sitting here for a while might be a good reminder. You can stay here until Connor gets his hat back."

Tyson knew that might be a long time. He slumped in the chair, thinking this whole thing was just getting boring now instead of funny.

As soon as the principal left, Mrs. Hardy looked at Tyson. "You should get a book."

Tyson got to his feet slowly. He looked at the clock and waited a minute for the morning break bell to ring. As the class in the library cleared out, Tyson snuck past Mrs. Chin. He technically wasn't allowed to take out books because he hadn't returned some from last year. Notices had been sent home, and Tyson's mom said it was his responsibility to either pay for the books or find them. He'd done neither, which put him in a tricky spot now.

His plan was to hide behind a shelf near the back of the room and wait for Mrs. Chin to leave for her break. As soon as she was gone, he'd snag a book and go back to the office.

He'd been waiting for a few minutes when he heard a voice. "Mrs. Chin, I'll just be a second. I have to check something." The student sounded breathless, like she'd run to the library.

"Go ahead, Jane," Mrs. Chin said.

From Tyson's hiding spot, he watched Jane cross the library to the chapter books. She looked over her shoulder once at Mrs. Chin, who was busy at her desk. Then Jane took a book with a blue cover off the shelf. She opened it, and he saw her face light up. She took two pieces of paper out of the book, grinning as she read the first one. Then she put one of the pieces of paper back and folded the other one and stuffed it in her pocket.

Tyson stayed hidden until he heard Jane talking to the librarian. "The book I wanted wasn't there."

Tyson thought about jumping up, and shouting *Liar, liar, pants on fire!* It would be funny, but it would blow his cover. He also wanted to know what was on the paper Jane had put back in the book. Was it possible Jane McDonald was up to no good? Tyson doubted it. Teachers probably arm-wrestled each other to get her into their classes.

Jane and Mrs. Chin had a quick conversation, and then Mrs. Chin turned off the lights and followed Jane into the hallway. The door shut with a muffled thud and Tyson was all alone. He stood up and looked around. He'd often dreamed of having a candy store to himself, or an amusement park, but never a library.

Tyson walked over to where Jane had been and scanned the shelves. She'd definitely been in the *S* section, middle row, but there were at least thirty books on the shelf. He positioned himself right where she had been standing and then looked for a blue book.

He pulled *Liar & Spy* off the shelf and shook it upside down. A piece of paper floated to the floor.

CHAPTER 9

Jane

Finding Sienna's note in *Liar & Spy* had made me want to laugh and cry at the same time. In the library, I'd quickly read the one addressed to me. Now, sitting in Mr. Lee's class for social studies, I held on to my heart pendant and read the note again.

Dear Jane,
Welcome to the Undercover Book Club! I know you miss me so much already (I miss you too!) and it feels like you'll never find another friend like me. Am I right?

Well, I came up with a brilliant plan, if I

do say so myself. We became besties because we both loved to read. I'm convinced that there are other kids at Forest Hills who feel the same way about books as you and me. The trick is finding them. We're very elusive!

There is another note here. It's for the next person who chooses to read this book. My theory is that you can find a friend based on similar reading choices—it makes sense, right? It's how you and I met!

Miss you already!

XO Sienna

P.S. Keep checking *Liar & Spy* for a reply! You never know when your book buddy will show up!

P.P.S. Your code name is X. You have to keep your identity a secret!

I looked around the class. Sienna had a lot more faith in the kids at Forest Hills School than I did. Sienna and I had found each other by luck, or maybe fate. Best-friend chemistry like ours didn't happen every day. We weren't a perfect combination just because we liked to do the same things, it was deeper than that. We were best friends because I trusted her with my secrets. She knew that when I throw a coin in a fountain, or blow out my birthday candles, I wish for my dad to come home and stay home. Besides my mom, Sienna was the only person I told when I got my period. She also knew I still slept with my stuffy, a dog named Snuggles.

I appreciated everything Sienna was trying to do with this note. A secret book club was something Safer from *Liar & Spy* would suggest. But if Sienna thought she was so easily replaced, she had another think coming.

Found it! I texted Sienna at lunchtime. She'd know I meant the note. I'd given the idea some more thought. I loved the idea of the Undercover Book Club—who wouldn't? But I also needed to be realistic. It might take days or weeks for someone to discover the note in *Liar & Spy*. And even if they did, they might not want to write back.

What if the person who found it was nothing like me? Or already had a best friend?

What if no one wrote back? I frowned, considering all the reasons the Undercover Book Club might fail. But a little voice that sounded a lot like Sienna's echoed in my head: *What if it succeeds?*

CHAPTER 10

Tyson

When Tyson got back to the office with the book he'd snuck out of the library, Mrs. Hardy told him to go to the conference room to read. As soon as he sat down he pulled the book out of his hoodie pocket and reread the typed note.

Hello!
I'm so happy you found my note! You're probably wondering what the heck is going on. Why is someone leaving notes in a book?

    I call it the Undercover Book Club and it's supposed to be a secret! We can leave notes and book recommendations for each other in *Liar & Spy*. I mean, it's kind of appropriate, isn't it? This book is all about solving mysteries (as you'll find out if you haven't read it yet) and now we have one of our own.

Hopefully, you love to read as much as I do. I can't wait to find out what book you suggest for me.

Sincerely,

X

Was this for real?

Jane's best friend, Sienna, had just moved away, so maybe this was Jane's solution for finding a new friend. It wasn't a very well-thought-out plan. Anyone could find the note. Like him, for example, and he was pretty sure he wasn't the type of person Jane had in mind for this weird club. She probably wanted someone as nerdy as she was. He tossed the book aside.

Except…the prankster in him couldn't resist. He didn't have to read the book to write back. She'd never know it was him anyway.

He ripped a piece of looseleaf out of his binder and tore it in half. Pressing hard with his pen, he wrote in tiny, neat letters:

Dear X,
I LOVE reading. I read all day, as much as I can. It's my favorite thing to do—more than stupid video games. This is one of my FAVORITE books. I've read it about thirty times.

From,

Thirty sounded impossible, so he crossed it out and wrote *lots* of instead. He bit the end of his pen thinking about how to sign the note. Obviously, he couldn't use his name. She'd signed *X*, so he did something similar.

Y

He thought about adding, *By the way, leaving a note in a book as a way to find a friend is never going to work* but then thought that was maybe a bit too mean.

She'd asked for a book suggestion, too. Tyson screwed up his face thinking. It had been a long time since he'd read a book. He didn't think she'd appreciate a *Diary of a Wimpy Kid* as a suggestion. When he had to read for school, he just picked anything off Mr. Lee's shelf and randomly flipped pages, reading a sentence here or there.

He could tell her to read the dictionary, or *Moby Dick*, but stringing her along a little might be more fun. The more serious his suggestion was, the more she'd believe that Y was real.

He thought back to sixth grade. Mr. Nucci had read them a book called *Harbor Me*. It had been about six kids who met up in an empty room, with no adults around, to talk about whatever they wanted. One kid's dad was in prison and another one's had been deported. It didn't have a lot of action, but Tyson had liked hearing about how each kid faced their struggles. He still thought about that book sometimes, a year later. Even though he'd pretended to be sleeping while Mr. Nucci read, he'd really liked it.

P.S. I think you should read *Harbor Me*.

He didn't know who the author was, but a nerdy girl like Jane could probably figure it out. Tyson slipped the note between the pages. He wished he could be there when Jane found his note. He imagined how excited she'd be, like a kid opening a present. The thought made him smile.

But for now, he was stuck in the conference room, staring at the beige walls. He tapped his feet on the floor, dug his thumbnail around the band on the table to see if it would peel off, and ripped a piece of paper into as many tiny pieces as he could, then blew them off the desk.

The clock on the wall ticked.

With nothing to do except stare at blank walls, he picked up the book again. Okay, the cover was sort of cool. Big buildings, just like in *Mutant-Z*. Maybe the book was about a battle. The title had the word *spy* in it after all. Sighing, Tyson opened the book, the paper heavy under his fingers as he turned to page one.

CHAPTER 11

Jane

Sienna and I were Mrs. Chin's Library Helpers. A few lunch hours a week, we'd help her shelve books. Lots of times she'd let us borrow a book before it was even catalogued if it was one we really wanted to read. Today though, I'd come to the library on a reconnaissance mission.

I went directly to the shelf where *Liar & Spy* was supposed to be. I blinked and looked again. Was I seeing right? The book was gone!

Someone had already taken it out. I couldn't wait to tell Sienna her plan was working.

Of course, whoever took out the book might be a slow reader, or maybe they hadn't started yet.

Sometimes kids took out books and stuffed them into their locker and forgot about them. The person who had *Liar & Spy* might return it next week without ever finding the note. If that happened, I'd have to go through the painful waiting period again as *Liar & Spy* sat on the shelf. "Mrs. Chin," I said, going to her desk. "I was looking for *Liar & Spy* by Rebecca Stead."

She moved to the computer. "Do you want me to put a hold on it?"

Asking who had the book out felt like breaking an unwritten rule of the Undercover Book Club. I didn't even know if Mrs. Chin would tell me because of privacy rules. "I just wondered when it's due back," I said. At least then I'd know when to check the shelves.

"Hmm," she said. "It hasn't been signed out. You're sure it's not on the shelf?"

Had I missed it? Mrs. Chin went to look but came back to the computer empty-handed. "I'll keep my eyes open for it. Maybe someone didn't put it back on the right shelf."

"Okay, thanks," I said.

"If you want a mystery, I just cataloged some new ones."

A pile of books sat waiting on the counter. I ran my hands over the spines, bothered that my detective skills were of no use when it came to solving who had removed *Liar & Spy* from the library.

CHAPTER 12

Tyson

Tyson lay on his bed. Without his Xbox, he had nothing to do. He didn't like the show Ava was watching in the family room, and the TV in his room didn't have cable since he only used it for playing video games.

Finally, with no other options, he dug out the book he'd started in the office. It surprised him to realize how much he'd read.

When Tyson's mom called him for dinner, he only had about fifty pages left. He was so wrapped up in Georges (the *s* is silent) and Safer's investigation of Mr. X that he didn't hear her.

"Dinner!" Ava said, bursting into his room.

He slammed the book shut and tried to hide

it under his pillow like it was something illegal, but he was too slow. She'd caught him. "What are you reading?" she asked.

"A book."

"Which one?"

"Stop being nosy," Tyson grumbled.

When Tyson and Ava got to the table, Max, and their parents were already seated. So far, there'd been no mention of a phone call from Mr. Morangi. Maybe he'd forgotten, or thought tossing Connor's hat on the roof wasn't a big enough deal to involve Tyson's parents. "What's for dinner?" Tyson asked.

"The lasagna we didn't have yesterday," said his mom with a pointed look in his direction.

"Heard you lost your Xbox," Max gloated. Tyson glowered at his fifteen-year-old brother, who was still sweaty from hockey practice.

"Shush, Max," their mom said. But that didn't stop Max from smirking at him.

"Max and I are going to watch a junior hockey game at the arena. The Blues are playing. Want to come?"

"You should go," his mom said. "Maddie and I are watching that celebrity dance competition on TV."

"Yeah. You don't have your Xbox, what else are you going to do?" Max asked. Tyson didn't have hobbies like Max and Ava did. And even though he had friends at Forest Hills, he didn't hang out with them outside of school. Andrew and Affan were always busy with basketball. Marcus and he gamed together sometimes, but without his Xbox, what would they do if he came over?

"I'll just hang out in my room, I guess."

"You could read," Ava suggested, flashing him a playful look.

Her comment made his mom burst out laughing. "Tyson? Read? I'd love to see that!"

His mom made it sound like it'd be a miracle if it happened. Tyson was surprised her comment stung as much as it did.

CHAPTER 13

Jane

True to her word, by Wednesday, Sienna had sent me a video of her new house. Her room did have an ocean view. A tiny sliver of blue-gray water was visible between the roofs of her neighbors' houses.

I showed it to Aisha, Grace, Dowoon, and Rafaella at lunch. "Looks nice," Rafaella said. "Did she start school yet?" Rafaella has the most gorgeous, thick, wavy brown hair. It looked so perfect against her olive skin she could be in a shampoo commercial. My own hair is a bushy dark blond mop, like Hermione's in the Harry Potter movies. "I could have helped her with outfit options."

"She starts today," I told them. Sienna was nervous and I wondered if she'd slept at all last night.

Emily, one of my Kid Lit Quiz teammates, beelined across the cafeteria to our table. Aisha groaned quietly under her breath. Emily was intense. She stopped at our table and peered at me through her small, round glasses like I was a specimen under a microscope.

"Stefan might quit the team," she blurted. "The science fair is coming up and he says he doesn't have time to work on his project *and* prepare for regionals."

Stefan, who was with Emily in the other grade seven class, loved fantasy, especially *Lord of the Rings*-type books. There were always a few genre-specific questions, so losing Stefan would put us at a disadvantage. He'd joined the team last year because he had a crush on Sienna. Now that she was gone, I wondered if he was using the science fair as an excuse to get out of the Kid Lit Quiz.

The Kid Lit Quiz season consisted of five tournaments. Teams had to have competed in the first four in order to be invited to the Super Book Invitational, aka regionals. The winning team went on to nationals. Trying to replace two players before regionals would be hard, especially since we didn't have a coach either.

Ms. Krauss had left Forest Hills a couple of weeks ago when her term position ended. She'd arranged for Mrs. Ng to coach, but then Mrs. Ng had to start her maternity leave early due to low blood pressure, which left us coach-less again.

I'd been so preoccupied with Sienna's move, planning her goodbye party, and then figuring out the clue she'd left for me, I'd let the Kid Lit Quiz fall off my radar. But Emily was right. Regionals were around the corner. It was time to get focused. We needed another team member and a coach, ASAP! "Tell Stefan he has to stick with it. We'll help him with his science fair project if we have to."

Just like for any competition, we had to train. Except our training meant reading. The trivia questions could be anything related to literature. Nursery rhymes, fairy tales, current bestsellers, myths, even Shakespeare! At each tournament, the Quizineer asked the teams 100 questions, divided into ten rounds. Points for correct answers were counted at the end of the tenth round and the three teams with the most points competed in the tournament final, and a winner was declared.

It was perfect for a book nerd like me.

"By the way, they announced where nationals are," Emily added. I waited for her to tell me. When she did, my jaw dropped. Sienna's new hometown!

For a second, I thought Emily was joking, but then I remembered, Emily never jokes. "We have to get our team together!" I said with renewed conviction. Going to nationals would mean seeing Sienna in person! "You convince Stefan not to bail on us. I'll look for someone to take Sienna's spot and find a coach."

Emily sighed and shook her head. "I'm not optimistic about our chances."

"For what?" I asked.

"Any of it," she replied, and walked away.

I looked at the girls I was sitting with. Aisha claimed reading was boring. She played soccer and liked to move, not sit and read. Grace and Dowoon were both shy. They liked reading, but the idea of answering trivia questions wasn't their idea of a good time. "How about you, Rafa? Do you want to join the team?"

Rafaella scrunched up her nose and shook her head, like I'd asked if she wanted to take a sip of spoiled milk. "So that's no?" I guessed.

"Sorry," she said. "I already have so much homework."

I shrugged her apology away. "It's okay. I'm sure we'll find someone." At least, I hoped so.

On the walk home from school, I thought about the Kid Lit Quiz team. If we could find a fourth team member and a coach, we would have a shot at winning regionals. We'd won the first tournament of the season and placed second in two others.

As Kate and I trudged up the driveway, I saw Grandpa sitting on the couch waiting for us.

Grandpa. Coach. Just like that, the two ideas collided.

Grandpa had time and was available after school when we practiced. He wasn't a teacher now, but he used to be one! Grandpa had taught middle school English before he retired. Mom was sure that was where I got my love of reading.

Why hadn't I thought of it before?

"Grandpa!" I said breathlessly as soon as I got into the house. "I need your help."

"What? What is it?" He must have got up too quickly because he had to hold on to the armrest of the couch to steady himself before he came over.

"I just had a great idea! Can you coach my Kid Lit Quiz team? You'd be perfect!"

Grandma and Grandpa had been to some of the tournaments. They knew how competitive they could be. Grandpa stuffed his hands in his pockets and rocked back and forth on his toes. "You're sure I'm the right guy?"

"Yes!"

I thought he'd take longer to think it over, but a second later he grinned and nodded. "Okay! I'm in!"

I threw my arms around him and squealed. "I'm going to call Sienna! She'll be so excited." I was halfway up the stairs before I remembered that Sienna wasn't on the team anymore. The excitement of finding a coach was replaced by a wave of missing my best friend.

CHAPTER 14

Tyson

Tyson stared at the book in his hands, hardly believing his eyes. He'd read it. The whole thing. In two days! Between the hours stuck in the conference room on Tuesday, and then the ones at home without his Xbox, he'd had nothing else to do but read.

He let the feeling of success sink in.

Now he had to get the book back into the library, not because he cared that much about returning school property, but he wanted to know what would happen when Jane found his note. Would she read his recommendation? Would she write back? He gave his head a shake. The Undercover Book Club was supposed to be just a joke. Another prank. Not something he actually cared about.

When Tyson got home on Thursday, *Liar & Spy* was still in his backpack. He'd tried to sneak it back onto the shelf at lunch, but Mr. Morangi had stopped him and asked him where he was going since the library was in the opposite direction of the cafeteria.

"I—uh—was going to he library. I wanted to get a book."

"Ha!" The principal laughed. "Nice try. Off you go. Find something to do that won't get you in trouble."

Tyson couldn't believe Mr. Morangi was telling him *not* to go to the library and *not* to get a book. Didn't that go against a teacher code of ethics or something? They were always hassling kids to read more. And now, he actually wanted to and Mr. Morangi was sending him away!

There had to be some way to return the book without drawing attention to himself. If he gave it to the librarian and said he had found it, she might discover the hidden notes. If he managed to slip it back onto the shelf, he wouldn't be able to check for a reply.

No, his best bet, he decided, was to find the overdue

library books that were somewhere in his house. If he returned them, Mrs. Chin would let him into the library anytime he wanted. Problem solved.

As long as he could find the books.

Ava was already home when Tyson arrived. She went to a different school, the one her friends from dance went to. She was lying on the couch with the TV on and her phone in her hands when Tyson walked through the room. Tyson glanced back at her before he slipped into her bedroom. She wasn't paying attention to him; her eyes were glued to her phone. He didn't want to explain why he was looking for overdue library books.

Tyson didn't go into Ava's room very often. It was painted salmon pink with a sparkly chandelier, and Tyson felt out of place as soon as he set foot inside. There were photos of Ava in dance competitions, doing gravity-defying feats, her toes pointed and legs stretched out so far they looked like she'd split apart. Rows of golden trophies sat on top of the bookshelf. Ava was the only one who had a bookshelf in her room, which was why Tyson thought the books might have ended up here.

He had no idea which books he was looking for. Maybe a *Captain Underpants*? What would he have picked last year for a book report he had no intention of writing?

And then he saw it. The library label on the spine gave it away. *Holes* by Louis Sachar. Mr. Nucci, his homeroom teacher last year, had pulled it off the shelf and slapped it against Tyson's chest. "This is the book for you," he'd said, and walked away. Tyson had taken it without even reading the back. But now he held the book in his hands and looked at it. Why had Mr. Nucci thought this was the book for him?

There had been another overdue book as well. Tyson ran his fingers along the spines hoping it would jump out at him. How had Ava got so many books? He barely ever saw her reading. But when he looked around her room, he noticed that a book was on her nightstand, a tasseled bookmark dangling out of it.

It wasn't until he got to the last shelf that he saw another library book: *Crossover* by Kwame Alexander. Mr. Nucci had recommended this one too. He let out a long sigh of relief and felt the corners of his mouth curve up. It had worked! Tyson almost couldn't believe it. He'd bring these books in tomorrow and put back *Liar & Spy* for Jane.

He took a look at *Holes*. He was curious about why Mr. Nucci had been so sure he'd like it. The rest of the night yawned in front of him. Since he couldn't play on his Xbox, he thought he might as well try reading another book.

"What are you doing?"

Tyson jumped and turned around. He'd been so focused on *Holes* that he hadn't heard Ava come in.

"Why are you in my room?" She looked at him suspiciously. "Are you looking for books?" she asked, seeing that he had two in his hands.

"Yeah. For a book report."

Ava bought the line. "Next time, just ask," she said, as he left her room with the books clutched in his hands.

CHAPTER 15

Jane

Emily nodded when I told her that Grandpa had agreed to be our coach. I'd already run it past Mr. Morangi. He loved the idea of Grandpa helping out and sent him an email outlining the paperwork that needed to be completed to make Grandpa an official Forest Hills volunteer coach. "Isn't that great?" I asked.

"Uh-huh," Emily said in a monotone. I'd been hoping for a little more excitement. Sienna's squeal had been so loud I'd had to hold the phone away from my ear, and she wasn't even on the team anymore! Her reaction to Grandpa coaching was nothing compared to what happened when I told her that nationals were in her new hometown. My ear drums were still vibrating.

"You *have* to win regionals!" she'd said. I completely agreed. Now that we had a coach, maybe we could.

Emily stared at me, her face expressionless. "But we're still down a player," she said. "Maybe two. Stefan won't commit."

"I'm working on it," I told her.

Well, first things first. Sienna had given me strict instructions to check the shelf for *Liar & Spy* daily. She wanted to know what would happen when it got returned. So did I! The mystery was killing me—was it a boy? A girl? Someone in my grade? And what book would they recommend?

I waved to Mrs. Chin as I passed her desk and went directly to the *S* shelf. I stopped an arm's length away from it, hardly believing my eyes. *Liar & Spy* was there! It was on the shelf!

As much as I wanted to jump up and down, I had to play it cool. I didn't want Mrs. Chin to get suspicious—not that she would care about the Undercover Book Club, I wasn't breaking any rules, but it was *secret* and I wanted it to stay that way, at least for now.

I pulled the book off the shelf and flipped through the pages. Sienna's note was still there, exactly where I'd left it. On the other side was more writing!

I squinted at the squished-together letters trying to make out what the note said.

Whoever had found it loved reading as much as I did and called themselves *Y*. I smiled. *X* and *Y*; we were like the unknowns in an equation. And, best of all, there was a recommendation for a book. I found *Harbor Me* by Jacqueline Woodson and skimmed the back cover as I brought it to Mrs. Chin.

"You've never read this one?" she asked.

I shook my head.

"It's very good."

I wanted to get right to it so I could plan which book I would choose next. I sized up the book as I went to my favorite cozy corner and sat down. Under 200 pages: it wouldn't take me long to finish it.

CHAPTER 16

Tyson

Tyson was at his locker, getting his stuff for the afternoon. Returning the book that morning had been such a relief. Jane had already gone by on her way to Mr. Lee's class. She was grinning and Tyson thought he saw *Harbor Me* in her hands.

This isn't a joke to her, he thought.

Two lockers down, Minju arrived, still flushed from basketball practice. She tossed in her gym bag. Tyson let his hair flop over one eye and sneaked a look at Minju. She was the prettiest girl in his class. Shiny, dark hair, and tall for her age. "Do we have math or English next period?" she asked.

"Yes," Tyson answered.

"So you have no idea?" she asked, smirking.

"Nope. I just show up." Minju gave him a good-natured laugh and grabbed her books. He thought she'd keep walking to Mr. Lee's class at the end of the hall, but she paused, waiting for him. Quickly, he took what he needed and slammed his locker shut.

"Your sister dances with mine. Did you know that? She came over the other day." This was news to Tyson. He wondered why Ava hadn't said anything.

"I was playing *Mutant-Z* and Ava said you're really good it."

Tyson gaped at her. "*You* like *Mutant-Z*?"

"Yeah, my stepdad got me hooked. I play whenever I'm at my mom's."

"What's your name? On the game, I mean."

"Talon."

Talon. Tyson repeated it in his head, imagining the Mutant that would go with that name.

"What about you?" Minju asked.

"Lizardo."

"Lizardo," she said under her breath, trying to place it. "Oh my God! I've played with you! You did this crazy move and almost got out of a factory you blew up!"

One side of Tyson's mouth turned down. *Almost.* That had been the day his mom had ripped the Xbox cable out of the wall. He imagined how much more impressed she'd have been if he'd managed to escape. "Oh yeah. You were in that game?"

"My stepdad got me to that level. I died really quick when I tried it on my own. Level nine is a killer."

They were almost at Mr. Lee's classroom. Tyson slowed his steps even more to delay their arrival. He wondered if he smelled bad. The shirt he was wearing had been lying on the end of his bed in a crumpled heap with other clothes—clean or dirty, he wasn't sure. It had never mattered until just now.

"Are you playing *Mutant-Z* tonight?"

He shook his head. "I'm grounded from my Xbox."

"Till when?"

"I'm supposed to get it back soon. Maybe this weekend." Tyson added a silent *hopefully*.

"Message me when you're on," Minju said.

Tyson brushed the hair out of his eyes and looked her square in the face. "Okay." He tried to sound as cool as possible, but inside he was high-fiving himself. *Minju Park wants me to message her!*

They made it into class just as the bell rang. Tyson sat down and even though most of him was thinking about *Mutant-Z* and Minju, a small part of him heard Mr. Lee tell everyone to get out their books for silent reading. As if he did it every class, Tyson reached into his backpack and pulled out *Holes*. When everyone else opened their books, Tyson did too.

CHAPTER 17

Jane

After school, Grandma and Grandpa were at the house. As soon as I walked in, I smelled baking. Grandma came to greet us at the door, giving out hugs like it was her job. There is no kind of bad day a Grandma-hug can't fix.

I took a deep breath. "Oatmeal chocolate chip?" I asked. She nodded, and we went into the kitchen. Grandpa was seated at the table and there were two plates already set out for Kate and me.

"I got a reply to the Undercover Book Club note," I told them. I'd been bursting to tell someone since I'd found it. "And a book recommendation."

"That's wonderful!" Grandma said, putting two cookies on my plate. "What's the new book?"

I pulled it out of my backpack and showed them. I was excited to finish it so I could write a note back to Y. Kate chatted about her day, but I ate my cookies quickly and downed a glass of milk. I wanted to get to upstairs and lose myself in the A.R.T.T. room of *Harbor Me*.

Right on schedule, the phone rang. Every Saturday morning at 10:00, Dad calls to check in. It was 8:00 p.m. where he was. He'd already finished dinner and we were just starting our day.

I pushed all that aside for now though because every second I could talk to Dad made him feel not so far away.

"Hey, Janey!" he said. "What's going on?"

For once, I had a lot to tell him. "Well, Sienna left," I said. "But she said her last day was the best worst day ever." I told him about the surprise and the gift I'd gotten her. I touched the heart pendant engraved with *Best Friend*. I'd worn it every day since she'd given it to me. "She left me a surprise too. I had to figure out a clue that led me to a book. Inside was a note." I paused dramatically. "Sienna started an Undercover Book Club for me."

"What's that?" Dad asked. I imagined him stretched out on the couch in his on-base accommodation. There were hundreds of other military personal stationed there, but as Chief of Staff he had a house to himself. "Me and whoever finds the note are supposed to write back and forth to each other with book recommendations. And guess what?" I asked, but didn't wait for him to answer, "Someone already did and I finished their book suggestion last night!"

"So you don't know who the other person is?"

"Not yet." The truth was I kind of liked the idea of Y being a mystery. For a while longer anyway.

"That's a great idea," Dad said. "Probably takes your mind off missing Sienna."

And missing you, I thought but didn't say. "What's going on there?" I asked. There wasn't much Dad told us about his job. He was in charge of lots of people and it was a big responsibility. It could also be dangerous. I'd learned the hard way that going online to look up the places my dad went was a bad idea. There was a reason they needed peacekeepers. Seeing the destruction, and knowing my dad was in the middle of it, filled me with worry. What if he got hurt? What if he was killed?

Mom always told me that Dad's job meant he wasn't near the actual fighting. He had a desk job that was more about organizing the soldiers and keeping the operation on-track than being in the middle of things.

But still, late at night when I couldn't sleep, my mind wandered to the worst-case scenarios.

"It's hot. Guess what I saw yesterday? A scorpion!" I am *not* a fan of bugs, and scorpions were in a whole demonic insect category I wanted nothing to do with.

"Are you telling me so I'll worry about poisonous insects instead of...other stuff?"

Dad laughed softly on the other end of the phone. "Maybe."

We both got quiet. "It's day 834," I reminded him. All the days he'd been away from me in my life added up to that number—almost two and a half years! Before he'd left this time, he'd promised me the number wouldn't go past a thousand.

"I know it is," he said quietly. "I'm counting too."

"I miss you," I said.

"I miss you too, sweetie."

Kate jumped up and down begging for the phone, so I said goodbye and passed it to her. Just like always, Mom was waiting with her arms open, giving me the hug Dad couldn't.

CHAPTER 18

Tyson

As soon as Tyson's mom walked in the back door on Saturday morning, loaded down with grocery bags, he asked, "Can I have my Xbox back?"

One bag slipped off her shoulder, dropping to her elbow. She passed him the laundry detergent and a jug of milk. "Help me put these away and I'll think about it."

Since yesterday, his thoughts had been preoccupied with Minju. He couldn't believe that she played *Mutant-Z*. Finally, he had someone to talk to about it.

"I haven't been in the principal's office since—" He broke off. "In a while." There was no point in bringing up the hat incident since Mr. Morangi hadn't called home. "And I read a book."

His mom snorted. "Yeah, right." She opened the fridge and put away the milk and orange juice.

"I'm serious. It was called *Liar & Spy* and I started another one called *Holes*."

"What was the spy book about?" she asked absently.

As Tyson told her the whole story, she stopped putting away groceries and listened, giving him one of those looks that made him wonder if he'd grown a second head.

"Tell you what. You read another book and I'll think about the Xbox."

"But you said I'd get it back today. I need it."

"Why? It sounds like things are going well without it. You're not getting in trouble and you're reading. It's a Christmas miracle."

"I promised someone I'd play with them."

His mom checked the time. "I have to get Ava from dance. Can you finish putting this stuff away? We'll talk about the Xbox when I get back."

Tyson gritted his teeth, but did as he was told. "And then, read," his mom told him before she left.

"I *have* been reading," he called to her, but she was already out the door. Once the groceries were put away, Tyson went to his room. He was more than halfway through the book. If he did nothing but read for the rest of the day, maybe he could finish it. And if he did, his mom would have to give him back his Xbox.

As he opened the book, he thought about Jane and the Undercover Book Club. Had she read *Holes?* If she had, he wondered if she'd figured out why the Warden was so intent on making the kids at Camp Green Lake dig holes.

CHAPTER 19

Jane

"Can I hang this up?" I asked Mrs. Chin. It was Monday morning and I'd worked on a Kid Lit Quiz recruitment poster over the weekend.

Love to Read? Join the Kid Lit Quiz Team!

Sign up in the library!

I'd used heavy cardstock and decorated the poster with books, golden stars, and question marks. I figured the bulletin board across from the library was the best place to advertise. Mrs. Chin said yes and handed me some thumbtacks. She took the sign-up sheet I'd made and taped it to her desk.

My morning library visit wasn't just to hang up the poster. I also wanted to leave a note in *Liar & Spy*.

I felt like a spy myself as I pulled the book off the shelf and opened it to the same spot Sienna had left the original note. I'd given my next book recommendation careful consideration. I waffled between *Front Desk* by Kelly Yang and a mystery called *The Parker Inheritance* by Varian Johnson. Finally I'd chosen *Wonder* by R. J. Palacio. It wasn't a mystery, but it was one of my favorite books. Sienna loved it too and had given it a thumbs up when we'd FaceTimed last night.

Being in the library, around so many of the books we'd shared, really made me miss her.

I touched my pendant and took a deep breath. Sienna was gone, but she was still just a phone call or a text away. If there was anything I'd learned from Dad and his absence, it was that the ache of missing someone came and went. Some days, I forgot Dad was half a world away and other days, it hit me like a punch to the gut. At least with Dad I knew there was an end date. I didn't know when I'd be with Sienna *in person* again. Which was why whipping the Kid Lit Quiz team into shape was so important. Getting to nationals wasn't just about competing against the best teams in the country. It was about being reunited with Sienna.

CHAPTER 20

Tyson

When Tyson put *Holes* on Mrs. Chin's desk, she looked at him, then at the book, then back at him. "What?" he asked.

"Did you read it?" she asked skeptically.

"Yeah. It was good. I *dug* it." He waited a beat. Mrs. Chin grinned at him. "I can take out another book, right?" he asked.

She nodded.

Tyson went straight to *Liar & Spy* and flipped through the pages. A new note was waiting for him. Jane wrote about how the characters in *Harbor Me* were all drifting through life, unsure of the future, until they realized they could count on each other.

It's cool that the book is called *Harbor Me* because they're all safe with each other, just like a harbor is a safe place for boats.

"Oh yeah," Tyson said quietly. Did all books have titles that meant something? He thought about *Holes*. Zero and Stanley dug them, but they were also in them—like people kept trapping them in holes. That was how he felt sometimes when a prank went too far and instead of just getting a laugh from his friends he got in trouble. He'd dug a hole so deep, he couldn't get out of it.

Tyson looked around the library. It was empty except for Mrs. Chin. He could hear her typing on the computer. He dug through his backpack until he found a pen and then he scribbled a note to Jane with a new book suggestion: *Holes* by Louis Sachar.

He found the book Jane recommended. *Wonder* was a lot thicker than the other two books he'd read. Tyson's stomach sank. He wasn't a fast reader like Jane. A book this long would take him months. Maybe the rest of the year.

The bell rang. With time running out before the second bell, he brought the book to Mrs. Chin's desk.

"This is a very good book," Mrs. Chin said as she

checked it out for him. "If you like that one, I've got others I can recommend."

"No thanks," he said. One person recommending books to him was plenty. He went to his locker and stuffed *Wonder* onto a shelf behind his gym shoes.

"Hi, Tyson."

He knew who it was without turning around. Minju. "Hey." His voice cracked and he cleared his throat to cover it. "I got my Xbox back. I messaged you." She hadn't replied though and Tyson had worried he'd misunderstood their conversation on Friday.

Minju sighed. "I'm at my dad's. He doesn't have an Xbox."

"Oh." So maybe he hadn't messed anything up.

"I want to play though. Could I come to your house?"

Tyson stared at her wondering if he hadn't heard her correctly. "Uh, yeah. Okay."

Minju flashed him a smile. "Great! When?"

Tyson blinked at her. He hadn't thought it would be that easy. "Uh, tomorrow?"

"Perfect!"

Minju left and Tyson got a flutter of nerves in the pit of his stomach. Had this really just happened?

In class, he glanced down the aisle to where Minju was talking to Connor, and then past them to Jane.

It was a good thing she sat on the other side of the room. She wouldn't be able to see the book he was reading was the one she'd suggested.

But even if she did see it, would it ever occur to her that Tyson was Y?

Mr. Lee gave the class a reading period before lunch. Tyson saw that Jane was reading *Holes* and she was almost finished. *Does she do anything else except read?* he wondered.

He needed to come up with another book suggestion. A longer one, to buy him some time while he read *Wonder.* Tyson twisted around in his chair as if he was stretching. His eyes fell on Minju. Her eyes were glued to the pages of her book. It was thick as a brick. Perfect.

"Minju," he whispered. She looked up. "What's the name of your book?"

She held up the cover so he could see: *The Book Thief.* Then she mouthed, *Why?*

He gave her a one-shoulder shrug, which he hoped came off as cool and nonchalant. He'd seen Max do the same thing when someone asked him about how his last game went. He let Minju go back to her reading and ripped a piece of paper out of his binder so he could scribble a note for Jane. At his next chance, he'd go to the library and hide it in *Liar & Spy*.

"I'm handing back your reading responses," Mr. Lee said when their silent reading period was over. He walked up and down the aisle depositing papers on kids' desks.

Usually Tyson had nothing to put in a reading response, so he doodled. His doodling skills had improved; his mark in English hadn't. But last class, when Mr. Lee had given them a prompt about characters, Tyson had had something to say. Once he'd started the response to *Holes*, it had been hard to turn off the words.

Mr. Lee paused at Tyson's desk and slapped the paper down. There were a few red marks adding in periods and capitals and a couple words were spelled wrong, but underneath Mr. Lee had written: *I'm glad you liked* Holes, *it's one of my favorite books too. I also loved how you noticed the theme and connected it with Zero and Stanley. You're right, ALL kids deserve a chance. Way to go, Tyson!*

Tyson stared at the paper. *Way to go, Tyson!* A smile spread across his face when he read the words. As soon as he got home, he was going to hang it on the fridge beside Ava's honor roll certificate and Max's Athlete of the Month award.

CHAPTER 21

Jane

I was in the library at lunch helping Mrs. Chin shelve books when I heard someone asking about the Kid Lit Quiz team.

My poster was working!

I ran over to Mrs. Chin's desk. A boy with black spiky hair was introducing himself to her as Hilman Banerji. "I just transferred here," he said.

"How old are you?" I asked. He could barely see over the circulation desk.

"Grade six! I'm very short for my age." He spoke in a quick staccato and got a dimple when he smiled.

"Do you know about the Kid Lit Quiz?" I asked.

He shook his head. "No, but I love to read."

"That's the most important part of training," I explained. I told Hilman about our team and that my grandpa was the coach. "Do you mind if I ask you some sample questions?" He followed me to a computer and I pulled up the Question Bank on the Kid Lit Quiz website. I started with some easy ones. "Who is Percy Jackson's father?"

Hilman gave me a blank stare. I moved on to the next one.

"Where does Katniss Everdeen travel to for the Hunger Games?"

Hilman shrugged. Maybe he was more into classics. I tried again.

"Who is Sherlock Holmes's investigative partner?"

"I don't know."

Oh boy. "One more," I said. "What kind of creature is Dobby?"

Hilman's face lit up. "A house elf! I've read all the Harry Potter books about ten times."

"Do you read anything else?" I asked. I was joking, but Hilman shook his head.

"No."

I hated to turn away a potential teammate, but we needed someone who liked a variety of books. "Look, Hilman. I'm really happy you want to be on the team.

We have some other kids interested, so we'll make our final decision next week." It was the nicest lie I could think of. I didn't want to get his hopes up, but we couldn't commit to someone who only read one author's books.

"Is there anything I could do, to you know, improve my chances?"

"Well," I started. "You could read books by other authors." I pointed out a few titles I thought he might like. By the time I was done, he had a stack in his arms for Mrs. Chin to sign out.

"One more thing," he said. "I have a very nervous stomach."

"Okay, thanks for letting me know," I said. I could see Mrs. Chin biting back a smile.

"How did it go?" she asked me after Hilman had left. When she saw my face she said, "Don't worry. You'll find someone."

I hoped she was right because missing the chance to see Sienna would be a major book-tastrophe.

I'd made it through another day without Sienna. I had a new book to read, thanks to Y. I'd finished *Holes* quickly, but *The Book Thief* was the kind of book I could get lost in.

I was curled up in my floof, which is a huge pillow that took up one corner of my room. There were other pillows piled behind my head and a goose-necked lamp for light and optimum reading comfort.

The time difference between here and Sienna's new home was making it hard to find a time to talk to her during the week. She'd just texted me that she'd been invited to a party.

Of course, I was happy for her. A party already! That was good news, but a little piece of me was jealous too. What if she found someone at her new school she liked better? I felt for the heart pendant and ran my fingers along the engraved words *Best Friend*.

Mom poked her head in my door. "Dinner's ready in a few minutes." She tilted her head at me. "You okay?"

"Uh-huh." She narrowed her eyes and "mommed" me. That is, she used her special mom mind control to make me admit something was wrong. There was no point fighting against it. I sighed and put my book down. "I miss Sienna." All of a sudden, there was a lump in my throat and tears sprang to my eyes.

"She's always a phone call away," Mom said.

Was she though? Between the time change and her new friends, what if we couldn't find time to talk? And now a party? "What if she forgets about me?"

"Oh, honey. Sienna couldn't forget you. She might make new friends, and you might make some too, but that's not going to take away who you are to each other."

"Everyone says that." I gave her a rueful look. "Are you still friends with the girls you hung out with in seventh grade?"

"Well, no, but that was thirty years ago. Anyway, I don't think I ever had a friend like Sienna."

There were other things bothering me too. I ran my finger along the seam of the floof wondering how honest I should be. "The Kid Lit Quiz team needs another person. One kid signed up, but I don't think he's a good fit. We can't go to regionals unless we have four people."

"There's still time. Someone else might sign up."

I nodded. The last thing was stuck in my throat. "And…I miss Dad." It was such a relief to say it out loud that I started to cry. I hated keeping all these things inside me.

Mom slid down from my bed to the floof and pulled me into a hug. She pressed me against her and let me sob onto her shoulder. "I know."

"It feels like people are always leaving me." In my head I rattled through their names: Sienna, Dad, even Ms. Krauss.

"It sucks, doesn't it?"

"Yes." I nodded. "It totally sucks."

Mom shifted so we were nestled together on the floof. "Dad's going to be home in a few months. And you'll get to see Sienna again. She's not going to forget you. How could she? You two are practically the same person."

"That's why it's so hard."

CHAPTER 22

Tyson

When Tyson got to homeroom on Tuesday, Mr. Lee was standing at the front of the room with a collection of locked metal boxes around him. "We're solving breakout kits today. You'll be working on problem solving, perseverance, and teamwork."

Mr. Lee held up one of the boxes. "For anyone who hasn't done a breakout kit, it's like an escape room. You and your partner will have to solve puzzles to open the locks and find out what's inside the box." Mr. Nucci had done breakout kits last year. Tyson hadn't helped his group. Instead, he'd hidden some of the clues. His partners hadn't found it funny when they discovered what he'd done.

"Can we pick who we work with?" Aisha asked.

Mr. Lee shook his head. "Nope, we'll leave it up to the Fates." Which meant he'd be picking names from his jar of Popsicle sticks.

Mr. Lee called out the first pair. "Grace and Connor," followed by, "Rafaella and Lucas." Rafaella motioned for Lucas to drive his electric chair over to her desk. The quiet hum of the motor filled the room until Mr. Lee called out the next name. "Tyson and…" Tyson kept his face neutral. *Please let it be Minju,* he thought. "Jane."

Tyson's eyebrows shot up in surprise.

After everyone's name had been called, Mr. Lee said, "Find your partners." Tyson looked over at Jane and reminded himself that as far as Jane knew, they were nothing but classmates. His side of the room was already more crowded, so he stood up and went to her, sitting down in the empty desk where Sienna used to sit.

"One person from each group, come and get a breakout kit," Mr. Lee said.

Neither of them moved. Then, "I'll go," they said at the same time.

"Jinx," Tyson said. Jane smiled.

"I'll go," Tyson said again, and stood up.

Minju was with a boy named Noah and she came

up to get a kit at the same time as Tyson did. "Is it still okay if I come over after school?" she whispered.

His cheeks got hot. "Yeah, I mean, if you still want to."

Minju's face lit up with a smile, which Tyson took as a yes.

His mom had made a new rule. He could only play on his Xbox for the same amount of time he read. She also took the controllers away before she went to bed, arguing that late-night playing was making him sleepy at school. Tyson told her it helped him relax, like taking shots in the driveway helped Max, but she just laughed and said, "You're twelve. What do you have to be stressed about?"

Actually, Tyson had a long list of things that stressed him out. Assignments that he didn't understand, tests, those lists that teachers wrote on the board with kids' names who hadn't handed something in. Those were the worst because then everyone could see all the work he hadn't done. On top of all that, now he had a hangout with Minju to worry about.

He wondered if other kids got stressed about things. With a start, he realized he could ask Jane in his next note.

Mr. Lee handed Tyson the kit and everything he needed. He took it all back to Jane.

"These are the clues. We have to figure out how they help." She read one, scribbling down possible answers.

One of the papers had a poem, and a letter in each line was bolded.

Solving the breakout kit felt a little like being detectives. Tyson thought of *Liar & Spy* and the two main characters who had to learn to trust each other to solve the mystery of Mr. X. "Do you think these letters are anything?" Tyson asked, pointing out the bolded ones.

"Maybe. You could write out all the highlighted letters in a row. See if they spell something. Or try to rearrange them—they might be scrambled."

Tyson nodded and got to work. "Oh, look," Jane said. "There's a question here." She showed him a different page. "Your word might be the answer to this."

Tyson copied out the letters down and focused on rearranging them.

CHAPTER 23

Jane

Working with Tyson wasn't as bad as I thought it would be. Last year, he'd sabotaged his team by hiding their clues. But this time, he was actually trying. We'd already got two of the locks open, but were stuck on the third one. That was when Tyson noticed something. "Hey, look." The instruction page was single-spaced, except for one line that was double-spaced. "That's kind of weird." I took what looked like a flashlight and turned it on.

It was a UV light and when I shone it on the paper, a sentence appeared. "Nice!" I whispered, and slid it across the desk so he could see. I couldn't help grinning. Solving puzzles like a breakout kit was right up my alley.

"What does it mean?" he asked.

I shrugged. "We have to go over the other clues to figure it out."

Minju walked by and did a double take when she saw how far along we were. "Wow! You're really good at this. We only got the first lock open." Minju grinned at both of us. Tyson's cheeks flushed.

Minju wandered back to Noah and Tyson kept working on the UV clue.

There was one lock left for us to open, but no more clues. "I've gone over every page," I said, frowning. "What did I miss?" Tyson looked around the class. Compared to the other teams, we were still doing the best. Most of them were only on the second clue.

"What about this?" Tyson asked. He held up a slip of a paper with a Harry Potter quote on it. "'We've all got both light and dark inside us. What matters is the part we choose to act on. That's who we really are. Sirius Black.'"

"That's from *Harry Potter and the Goblet of Fire*. Mr. Lee's a Potterhead, too," I said.

"A what-head?" Tyson asked.

"A Potterhead. You know, a Harry Potter fan."

"That would explain all the posters," Tyson said.

I'd thought it was a "red herring," which means a fake clue, but then Tyson grabbed my pencil and wrote

2000 on the scrap paper. "Look." He motioned with his head toward the *Goblet of Fire* poster on the wall. Underneath was the book's release date—the year 2000. Could that be the four-digit number we were missing?

"Try it!" I said. If Tyson was right, we'd have this breakout kit finished in record time.

Tyson reached for the last lock on the box and spun it so the numbers read *2000*.

The lock opened. "Done!" He shouted it so loudly, even I jumped.

Mr. Lee was helping another group and turned to see who had yelled. When he saw Tyson holding the open lock in his hand his face broke into a grin. Tyson didn't bother to check what was inside. I guess being in the first group to open the breakout box was prize enough.

That evening, I read Y's note over the phone to Sienna.

Dear X,
I really like *Wonder*. I like the parts where Auggie is in the space helmet. I wish I had one of those to hide behind sometimes. I also hope if I met a kid like Auggie, I'd be nice to him.

On the other end of the phone, Sienna went, "Awww."

"There's more," I said and kept reading.

> You know how in *Holes* people wrote Zero off as being stupid and not good at anything but digging holes? I think sometimes we do that to people in real life. There's lots we don't know about people. We only see one side of them and then try to put them in a box. Kind of like how the boys in the book were stuck in holes. Sometimes, it's easier to just stay there than climb out.
>
> See ya, Y

I waited for Sienna to say something. "What do you think?" I prompted.

"Is that the whole note? There's no book suggestion?"

"No. That's it."

"I think Y sounds…lonely. Do you think Y is a boy or a girl?" Sienna asked. I'd been wondering the same thing.

"I'm trying not to stereotype, but their writing is kind of messy—"

"So is Aisha's," Sienna pointed out. Aisha was always in a rush. The teachers insisted she type her work. "And Connor has the nicest printing of anyone. That's not a clue."

"Okay," I agreed. "The books Y's suggested don't give anything away either. They could be a boy or a girl. I wonder what they think I am." I had done a good job of keeping my books gender neutral too. Not on purpose, I just liked books that appealed to everyone. "What do you think I should say?"

"You could offer to meet," Sienna suggested.

I'd been thinking the same thing. I hated the idea of Y needing a friend, especially when I was right here. "Or"—Sienna paused dramatically—"you could invite Y to be on the Kid Lit Quiz team!"

The posters had been up for two days and the only kid who'd been interested was Hilman. The way Sienna's voice got high-pitched with excitement told me she thought her idea was a winner, but I wasn't so sure. Joining the Kid Lit Quiz team came with pressure. "What if it scares them away?"

"They can say no and still be part of the Undercover Book Club."

With that thought in mind, I hung up with Sienna to work on my note. I'd put it in *Liar & Spy* tomorrow and hope for a reply soon. With regionals only weeks away, we needed to start training.

CHAPTER 24

Tyson

Tyson had been worried about not having anything to talk about with Minju on the walk home. Minju was different than his other friends. Talking about pranks didn't impress her, and he knew she wouldn't think the fact that he'd answered every question on their last math test with *Your mama* as hilarious as Andrew had.

Luckily, Minju did enough talking for both of them. She knew a lot about other kids in the class and filled Tyson in on some gossip. Who like-liked who, who didn't like-like who and who like-liked who but who didn't like-like them back. It was all very confusing. "So, do you think your brother will be home?" Minju asked a block from Tyson's house.

Tyson frowned at her. "I don't know. Why?"

"Just, you know, wondered." She kept the tone light, but there was a glint in her eye that Tyson hadn't noticed before.

When they arrived at his house his shout of "Hello?" went unanswered.

"Aren't you going to show me around?" Minju asked when they got through the kitchen to the hallway.

He swung his arms up and out. "Not much to see."

Minju began a self-guided tour anyway. All Tyson could do was follow her. When they were in the living room, she looked at all the family photos as if committing them to memory. She wanted to know which little boy was Max and which one was Tyson. He tried to pretend it didn't bug him that she spent more time looking at the ones of Max.

"You don't want to go in there," he said when the tour moved toward Max's room. "Unless you have a Hazmat suit." Max's room stunk like gym socks.

Minju shrugged. She gazed around the room and its shelves of hockey trophies with wide-eyed curiosity.

"Do you want something to eat?" he asked.

"Sure." Reluctantly, she left Max's room. They were in the kitchen when he heard a car pull into the attached garage. A moment later, the back door opened. Tyson's mom and Ava walked in.

"Hi, Tyson," his mom said. She looked at Minju in surprise. "I didn't know you were having a friend over."

Minju gave Tyson's mom a megawatt smile. "I'm Minju. Hayeon's sister."

Realization dawned over his mom's face. "Oh! Nice to meet you."

"Minju likes *Mutant-Z*," Tyson explained. "We were gonna play for a while." He hoped his mom wouldn't mention the "read first" rule.

Minju waved at Ava. "No dance class today?"

Ava shook her head. She looked at her brother and back to Minju as if she couldn't make sense of the two of them together.

"Let's go play before you have to leave," Tyson said, and left the kitchen, walking toward his room. They got as far as the hallway when Max opened the front door and wheeled his gear in. The stench made Tyson wrinkle his nose, but Minju paused as if it was the sweetest perfume.

She nudged Tyson. "Aren't you going to introduce me?"

"Max, Minju. Minju, Max." Max gave her a chin nod and Minju's face lit up. Like he always did, Max went directly to the kitchen. He ate more in a day than the rest of them combined.

Minju followed him with her eyes. "You know, I am kind of hungry," she said. Without waiting for Tyson, she went back toward the kitchen. Tyson was no relationship expert, but he was starting to understand the situation. Minju liked him, but she *like-liked* Max.

It was crowded with all of them in there, but Minju didn't mind. She'd managed to move beside Max. Tyson had opened his mouth to ask her what she wanted for a snack when she said, "Hey Max, how's your hockey team doing?"

Max was always happy to talk about that. He was captain and led the team in points. As Minju leaned forward to listen to his answer, Tyson realized he couldn't compete with Max, Mr. Athlete of the Month. Unless…an idea started to percolate in his head. Minju liked Max because she thought he was cool. But what if he showed her the real Max. The Max only his family saw.

While Minju peppered Max with questions, Tyson snuck back to his brother's room. He lifted up the pillow on his bed and found Whiffer, the stuffed dog that Max still slept with. It was as old as Max and had been washed so many times, most of the stuffing had clumped up in the paws. He couldn't wait to see the look on Minju's face when he paraded into the kitchen and explained where the stuffy had come from.

"Ty?" He turned around, hiding Whiffer behind his back. Ava looked at him from the doorway. She took in the flipped over pillow and rumpled bed. "What are you doing?"

Tyson smirked.

Ava gasped. "You're not going to show Whiffer to Minju!"

There was no point in denying his plan. "It'll be funny," he said.

Ava shook her head. "No, it won't be. Think about it, Ty. Do you really want to do that Max?"

The answer was: yes, that was exactly what he wanted to do. His brother was great at everything— school, hockey, and impressing girls. It wasn't fair. Just once, Tyson wanted to be the star.

"Embarrassing Max won't make Minju like you. It'll just make you look like a jerk. Besides, high school guys aren't interested in seventh-graders. No matter how cool Minju is."

"Then why is Minju out there talking to him?"

Ava looked at him, exasperated. "Because you're in here with Max's stuffy!"

Tyson sat down on the bed, deflated. She was right. As soon as he saw Minju paying attention to Max, he'd bailed. But he couldn't rival Max. He may as well hide in his room until Minju left. She probably wouldn't even notice.

"Look," Ava said, taking pity on him. "You and Minju both like *Mutant-Z*, right?" Tyson nodded. "And you're really good at it. Max isn't."

Tyson thought about this. "So I shouldn't embarrass Max. I should annihilate him."

"Not the way I would have worded it but you have the right idea. Bring your Xbox into the family room and challenge him to a game. You and Minju can be a team. I'll play with Max."

Tyson looked at Ava, wondering how she got so smart. Whiffer went back to his hiding place under the pillow and Tyson went to his room. He yanked the cables for the Xbox out of the wall, carried the whole thing to the family room and started attaching the console to the back of the big-screen TV.

"What are you doing?" Max asked wandering into the family room. Tyson glanced over. Minju was there too.

"Let's play," he said. "Together." Minju sat down and grabbed a controller. She logged in as Talon. Ava and Max joined them.

Max looked between Tyson and Minju, a slow smile spreading across his face. "Take it easy on me, okay? I'm not as good at this game as Ty."

"No promises," Minju said and grinned at Tyson.

Once the four of them started playing *Mutant-Z* together, Minju stopped drooling over Max and started behaving like her normal self. Just like on the basketball court, she played to win. Tyson showed off his skills too, and taught Minju some new tricks. Max and Ava sat back and watched, until Max disappeared into his room. Minju was so into the game, she didn't even notice. Ava's plan had worked perfectly.

CHAPTER 25

Jane

I had the note pressed in my palm when I walked through the library doors. The poster I'd made was still on the bulletin board. I didn't want to hurt Hilman's feelings but getting to the nationals was going to require the best team I could find. In my heart, I knew someone like Y would be perfect.

Y read widely and connected to books only the way someone who loved to read could—look at the insights they'd had about Auggie in *Wonder* and the boys in *Holes*.

I read the note one more time, making sure I hadn't given away my identity in case Y said no. I'd written:

Have you heard of the Kid Lit Quiz team? They compete in trivia competitions based on books. With all the reading you do, you'd be perfect! FYI, they have a practice after school on Thursday in the library. You should go!

I tucked the note into *Liar & Spy*. "Please say yes," I whispered. How funny it would be if Sienna's original note brought Y and me together, and then Y joined the Kid Lit Quiz team, helped us win, and then brought Sienna and me together if we won regionals! It would be a win-win-win!

I left the library feeling hopeful and excited for Y's reply.

The good feeling lasted all of ten seconds before I heard Andrew's loud laugh. He, Affan, and Tyson were standing by the poster I'd made. They were having too much fun to just be looking at it. I walked closer and when Affan moved away I saw what they thought was so funny.

They'd drawn penises all over the poster!

Affan noticed me and tugged on Andrew's arm. "Wait, one more," he said as he reached up with the Sharpie and drew another one in the top corner.

I stared at the boys. Tyson was the only one who looked embarrassed that he'd been caught. The rest of them thought it was hilarious that a poster I'd worked so hard on was ruined.

CHAPTER 26

Tyson

As far as school posters went, the one advertising the Kid Lit Quiz team was a work of art. The title was in multicolored bubble letters. Color copies of book covers had been cut out and dotted the background. There were also small gold stars to give the poster some sparkle. Someone had spent a lot of time on it.

Now it was ruined because Andrew had drawn weird, misshapen penises all over it.

Affan and Andrew were in hysterics. Tyson kept an eye on the door to the office. The last thing he wanted was to get caught.

The penis game had been his invention and it had been going on for a few weeks now. The goal was to draw as many penises as possible before the risk of discovery forced the vandal to walk away. The penis drawings looked nothing like the real thing. Done quickly, they were just an oval flanked by two circles at the base, but the seventh-grade boys all knew what the drawing was. Most of them had found one on their binder, pencil case, or even a textbook.

None of them had been bold enough to do a drawing this public before. Encouraged by his friends' reactions, Andrew did another and another.

"What are you doing?" Jane asked.

Andrew let loose a loud, honking laugh. "Nothing."

Jane's face went crimson. "That's my poster," she said. She took a few steps closer, her arms stiff at her sides.

"Stop it," Tyson said. Hearing the words come out of his mouth surprised him as much as they did everyone. He grabbed the marker out of Andrew's hand.

"Mr. Flamand!"

Tyson turned. Mr. Morangi had stepped out of his office. "What's going on?"

As if they were one person, Andrew and Affan took a giant step away from Tyson. He was left holding the marker in front of Jane's penis-dotted poster. Mr. Morangi took in the scene and pointed to his office.

CHAPTER 27

Jane

"It wasn't Tyson." I was as surprised as anyone to hear the words come out of my mouth. Mr. Morangi turned to me, then looked at the three other boys. He raised one eyebrow suspiciously.

"Fine. *All* of you, in my office."

I waited for Tyson to proclaim his innocence, but he didn't say anything. So I stepped in. "Tyson grabbed the marker from Andrew to stop him. Tyson didn't do any of the drawings."

"Let me get this straight. Tyson was *not* involved in this prank?"

It was hard for me to believe too, but it was the truth.

Mr. Morangi held his hand out for the marker. Tyson gave it to him. "Off you go, Tyson. You two, follow me."

Affan muttered that he'd just been standing there, the same as Tyson, but when Mr. Morangi asked if he'd done anything to stop Andrew, he had to admit he hadn't. Tyson and I watched as the two of them were escorted into Mr. Morangi's office.

"Sorry about your poster," Tyson said.

I looked at the ruined poster wondering if it could be salvaged. "You could print out a few more book covers and glue them on top of the drawings," Tyson suggested.

I'd need a lot of book covers. "The poster wasn't doing much good. Only one person signed up."

"What is the Kid Lit Quiz team, anyway?"

"It turns reading into a sport," I said, quoting from the website. "We go to tournaments and answer questions about books."

Tyson looked at me like I was joking. "And that's fun?"

"Yeah," I said, defensively. "To me it is."

"How do you practice? Just sit around and read?"

I nodded and took down the poster. I wasn't in the mood to answer any more of his questions. He was only asking so he could tease me. At least that was what I thought. When I looked at him from the corner of my eye, he wasn't smirking. He actually looked interested. "How many more people do you need?"

"I mean, technically, none since Hilman signed up. But I'm not sure he's ready to compete yet. All he's read is Harry Potter. I really thought more people would be interested. We were second at regionals last year. Whyte Ridge Middle School beat us, so they got to go to nationals."

"It's like a real thing, with a national competition?" Tyson asked.

I nodded. "The winning team has to pay for their travel costs. Usually they fundraise and ask for donations. The Kid Lit Quiz organizers help too. I was really hoping to get to nationals. It's in the same city that Sienna moved to. It would have been my chance to see her."

I stuffed the poster into the recycling bin in the hallway with a sigh. *Not much chance of that happening now.*

"Jane." Mr. Morangi stepped out of his office. "Andrew and Affan will be making new posters for you. Penis-free posters," he clarified. "Would you tell me what information they need to include?" He gave me a sticky note and I wrote down the details. Part of me wanted to tell Mr. Morangi not to bother. What was the point in making new posters if no one was interested in joining?

When I was done and had given the sticky note back to Mr. Morangi, Tyson was nowhere to be seen.

With the Kid Lit Quiz regional tournament quickly approaching, we needed to get our team in tip-top shape. We could not lose to Whyte Ridge Middle School again. Just thinking about the smug smile on the face of their captain made me want to vomit.

"Grandpa, I think we should have a Kid Lit Quiz team practice." Who knows, maybe Hilman would surprise me. "How does tomorrow sound?"

Grandpa's face lit up. "Sure." His eyes slid to Kate, who was working on a puzzle with him.

"I already cleared the practice with Mrs. Chin. She said we could use the library." Kate would have to stay too, but there were plenty of books for her to read, plus a Lego wall and some other bins of construction toys.

"Any new recruits?" he asked.

One other person had asked, but they were going on a family vacation at the same time as regionals. Two fifth-graders had also been interested, but players had to be in grades six to eight. I was holding out hope that someone else would step forward to join us. I still wasn't 100% sold on Hilman as our fourth teammate. We could put him on the roster as an alternate, but he needed to read more than Harry Potter if he wanted to compete.

The rules about the team members were clear. There had to be four people at the team table, plus a coach who sat in the audience during the tournament. Having an alternate was encouraged, in case someone didn't make it, but once the meet started, substituting players wasn't allowed.

"I left a note for Y asking if they want to join," I told Grandpa.

"I thought it was supposed to be a *secret* book club. Not much of a secret if they join the Kid Lit Quiz team."

"I know, but I'm desperate."

I had to admit, I'd miss the thrill of having a secret book buddy. There was a lot of freedom in writing letters to someone anonymously. I wondered if Y felt the same. There was no telling who he or she was. Other than the fact that they liked to read, they could be anyone at Forest Hills.

The trade-off for saying goodbye to Y was saying hello to a friend and maybe a Kid Lit Quiz teammate.

CHAPTER 28

Tyson

"Have you ever heard of the Kid Lit Quiz?" Tyson asked Ava that evening after dinner. They were watching YouTube on the TV in the family room.

"The trivia thing? Yeah, we have a team at school." Ava looked over at Tyson. "Why?"

"Just wondering."

Ava scrolled through her phone. "My teacher asks us questions from the website sometimes. You want to try some?" She didn't wait for his answer. "'What type of dress did Angelina Ballerina wear?'"

Tyson rolled his eyes. "Is that actually a question?"

Ava laughed and nodded. She'd been obsessed with Angelina Ballerina, a mouse who loved ballet, when she was little. Tyson had had to sit through more episodes than he could count. "A tutu," he said

"Next one. 'What is the only thing the BFG eats?'"

It was like the questions were rigged. His third-grade teacher had read them Roald Dahl's *The BFG*. "Snozzcumbers!"

"Right!" Tyson answered two more questions correctly, but got stuck on "What book by Charles Dickens was famous for its portrayal of criminals and their nasty lives?" The answer was *Oliver Twist*, but Tyson had never heard of the author or the book.

"You're good at these," Ava said. "You should join the team."

The note Jane had left today suggested the same thing. "Me?"

"Why not?"

He fixed her with a look. His own mother was still in shock that he was reading. What would Andrew say? Or Affan? Tyson was the last person they'd expect to join the Kid Lit Quiz team. "You know why."

She rolled her eyes. "Who cares what people think?"

"The team wouldn't want me."

"How do you know unless you ask? If you get the next question right, you have to go to the next practice. Deal?"

Tyson nodded, reluctantly.

"What stuffing was used inside the little boy's beloved Velveteen Rabbit?"

It was a story his mom had read to them many times when he was little. He looked at Ava and considered saying the wrong answer to end the discussion.

But he thought of that poor rabbit and how desperately he wanted to turn into something else. There was a slight catch in his throat when he gave the correct answer. "Sawdust."

CHAPTER 29

Jane

I waited with Kate in the hallway as Grandpa signed in at the office. Emily and Stefan were in the library. So was Hilman. I was glad to see him. I hadn't received a reply from Y, which meant Hilman was our fourth member.

Grandpa got a *Guest* badge from Mrs. Hardy and followed Kate and me to meet the rest of the team. Kate tugged on my sleeve. "I need to go to the washroom," she said.

"So go."

"I don't know where they are." The primary kids didn't come to the middle school part of the building very often. I sighed and excused myself as Grandpa started introductions.

A few minutes later, as Kate and I were heading back to the library, I noticed someone hanging around outside.

It was Tyson. He was pacing back and forth, like he wanted to come in. Had the doors been locked already?

I pushed the door open and stuck my head outside. A gust of chilly air hit me. "Do you need something?"

"I was…ah…Isn't your practice thing today?"

"The Kid Lit Quiz? Yeah. We just started."

"Did you find another person?"

"No." I sighed. "But with Hilman we have four."

Tyson shuffled from foot to foot nervously. Something was definitely up, but I didn't know what.

"That's why I'm here."

I blinked at him, hardly believing my ears. "You're here for the Kid Lit Quiz practice?"

He took a deep breath. "Yes."

It took me a second to process this news. Tyson Flamand wanted to join the Kid Lit Quiz team? "Are you—is this for real?" The last thing the team needed was a prank.

But I didn't think he was joking. He knew how much making it to nationals meant to me. Tyson might make some impulsive decisions, but he wasn't mean. He swallowed nervously and nodded. "That's great!" I said, hoping I didn't look as shocked as I felt. "Come on in."

I'd been surprised by his appearance, but it was nothing compared to the look on Emily and Stefan's faces when we walked into the library. "What's he doing here?" Stefan asked.

"Tyson wants to join," I said. I'd thought Hilman might be upset, but he looked relieved.

Stefan and Emily exchanged a skeptical look. I introduced Tyson to Hilman and Grandpa. "Call me Coach Albert," Grandpa said. "Or Coach Grandpa." He winked at me. "Ready to get started?"

All of us, including Tyson, nodded.

CHAPTER 30

Tyson

Tyson's nerves got the better at him for the first practice round. He didn't get any of the questions right. But neither did Hilman, so that made him feel better. The second round was supposedly harder, but he got three out of ten right.

Jane smiled at him. He was sitting across from her at the table. "For this round, we'll play as if it's a real competition," Coach Albert said. "Emily, Stefan and Hilman, you three work together. Jane and Tyson, you can partner up." Each team had a paper in front of them. After Coach Albert read the question, they'd have one minute to discuss, write, and answer.

"At a real competition, we'll be sitting near to

the other teams. We should get used to whispering," Emily said.

"First question: Which J.R.R. Tolkien dragon is described as being a 'greedy, strong, and wicked worm'?"

Jane didn't know the answer. "I don't like fantasy," she whispered to Tyson. She was about to draw a dash on the blank space to indicate they had no answer, but Tyson stopped her.

Every winter break, his family had a Lord of the Rings movie-a-thon. They watched all five films, in the correct order. He remembered the dragon's name. "It's Smaug." Jane looked impressed and wrote it down.

They both knew the answer to the next question: "What is someone who can't read or write called?"

Illiterate.

"Who are Nancy Drew's two best friends?"

Bess and George, Jane wrote, without conferring with Tyson.

"Where do Stanley and Zero meet?"

"Camp Green Lake," Tyson answered quickly. "In Texas." Jane nodded because she knew that one too.

"What do the Wild Things threaten to do to Max because they love him so?"

Everyone was stumped. "Can you repeat it, please?"

Stefan asked. He was a mouth-breather and his exhalations got even louder when he was concentrating.

As Coach Albert read the question again, a memory popped into Tyson's head. It was of his mom reading to him before bed. He could see the book and hear her voice. He squeezed his eyes shut. She'd tickle him every time she said it. Under his breath he mumbled, "We'll eat you up, we love you so."

He looked at Jane. She looked at him and her face broke into a smile.

I can do this, Tyson thought.

CHAPTER 31

Jane

"How'd the Kid Lit Quiz practice go?" Dad asked when we talked on Saturday.

Mom, Kate and I were cuddled on the couch and Dad was on speaker so we could all hear him. "Two people joined," I told him. "Tyson and Hilman. Tyson is in my class."

Dad didn't know the kids in my class well enough to realize how surprising it was that, of all kids, *Tyson* was the one who had shown up. Sienna had stayed silent for a full minute when I'd told her. Then she accused me of pranking her. "I would not lie about this," I'd promised. She made me swear on my collection of Enola Holmes books that it was true.

"Was he any good?" Dad asked.

"He was!" Hilman, on the other hand, hadn't been joking about his nervous stomach. He'd had to leave the library twice to deal with it.

"When's the first tournament?" Dad asked.

"In thirteen days."

"I wish I could be there," he said. I could hear the longing in his voice. A once-a-week phone call was a nothing compared to seeing Dad every day.

"Me too."

"Five more months, Janey. And then I'll be home."

"That's still really long time." I sighed.

"I know, but it'll go by fast. I mean, you've got your tournament to look forward to, and then summer holidays." I was familiar with the list-of-upcoming-events strategy. Both my parents used it. They thought distracting me with other things would make me forget that Dad's homecoming was still months away. "Anyhow, what would Mom do if I was home all the time?" Dad joked.

"She'd say it would be a nice problem to have."

Dad gave a soft laugh and changed the subject. "Any news on your book buddy?"

"You mean Y? Well, they never showed up to the Kid Lit Quiz team." I was disappointed, but in the end it hadn't mattered. Tyson was a surprisingly good addition. With Hilman in training as our spare, I felt confident that with or without Y, we weren't going to embarrass ourselves at regionals. Were nationals within our reach? We had two more weeks to find out.

CHAPTER 32

Tyson

Tyson glanced at his Xbox as he got ready for school on Monday. It used to be hard to leave it every morning. He didn't feel that way anymore. He'd played for a while last night with Minju, which had been fun, but getting to the next level and beating the other online players didn't matter as much as it had.

"Tyson," Ava shouted his name, breaking it up into two sing-song syllables. She burst into his room. "You're awake!" she said, surprised. Ava looked around his room. Her eyes landed on *Wonder*. It was on his nightstand. "Is that what you're reading?" she asked.

"Not anymore. I finished it last night." He didn't bother hiding his pride. It hadn't even taken him as long as he thought it would. He was hoping to read at least one more book, maybe two, before the tournament. He had eleven days—could he do it?

"Who's giving you all these books?" she asked. "Your teacher?"

Tyson almost nodded to avoid the truth. But at the last minute changed his mind. If there was anyone he could trust with this secret, it was Ava. "Actually, it's this girl, Jane." As Tyson launched into the whole story about the Undercover Book Club, Ava's eyes widened.

"Ty! That is so cool!" she said when he was done explaining. "And now you've both read all these books. You have an Undercover Book *List*!"

"She's also on the Kid Lit Quiz team," Tyson said.

Ava narrowed her eyes at him. "Did you join?"

"I went to the practice last week." He still couldn't believe he was doing something so nerdy…and liking it.

Ava beamed at him. "How was it?"

"It was okay," he said, playing it cool. But really, it had been better than okay. He'd had a great time.

"And she has no idea who you are?"

"No." Tyson was sure of it.

"When are you going to tell her?"

"I'm not," Tyson said. *Ever.*

Ava gaped at him. "She left the letters to find a friend. You can't leave her hanging!"

Downstairs, Tyson's mom yelled at them to hurry up.

Tyson put *Wonder* into his backpack and slung the bag over his shoulder. Ava stood in front of him, blocking his way out. "Promise you'll think about it."

Gently, he shoved her out of the way. Ava had been right about Minju. And about joining the Kid Lit Quiz team, but she was wrong about the Undercover Book Club. Jane liked Y because Y shared things Tyson couldn't. Admitting that he was Y would ruin things; Jane might stop leaving notes if she knew he was Y.

He didn't know when or how it had happened, but The Undercover Book Club mattered to him. He didn't want to risk losing it.

When Tyson got to school, he went straight to the library. He had a new note to leave for Jane.

Dear X,
I play this game called Mutant-Z. Have you heard of it? The players pick characters, either human or mutants. I'm a reptile named Lizardo. When I'm Lizardo, I'm not afraid to take risks. I help the other

mutants. Sometimes it feels like Lizardo is the real me, and the real me is actually the fake me.

Tyson had given the next thing he wanted to say a lot of thought. He'd never admitted it before and putting it on paper had felt like a leap. Like when Lizardo had to jump between buildings and he didn't know if he could make it. *I can always rip up the note*, he thought. But once he'd started writing, it felt like a hundred-pound weight had been lifted off his shoulders.

The person people see isn't the real me. It's someone I hide behind. I guess it is because I'm scared that people won't like the real me. When you asked me to come to the Kid Lit Quiz practice I got scared. What if I came and you were disappointed? What if you were hoping I'd be someone different? So that's why I didn't show up. I hope you can understand.

Y

He'd left room at the end of the note to add a book suggestion. Knowing Jane, she'd need a new one. His eyes landed on a book Mrs. Chin had put on display.

The line beneath the title said, *An unlikely friendship*. That pretty much summed up how things were for him and Jane. The book was called *Hello, Universe* by Erin Entrada Kelly.

Last week, she'd suggested *Bloom* by Kenneth Oppel. Tyson skimmed the back cover. An alien plant species and three kids who have to fight them? It sounded like the premise for a video game. He grabbed the book and went to Mrs. Chin's desk.

"Have you read all the books in the library?" he asked.

"Not all of them. But a lot."

"What's your favorite?"

"That's a hard one." She sighed. "I really like all of Susin Nielsen's books. You'd probably like them too. They're very funny. Her latest one is excellent."

"Can you put a hold on it for me?" He'd heard other kids ask her to do that, but it still sounded weird coming out of his mouth.

Mrs. Chin bit back a smile. "Of course I can." She typed a few things into her computer. "Done! I'll let you know when it's in."

Tyson looked at the clock. The first bell hadn't rung yet. He could take his time getting his binder from his locker without worrying about being late. Andrew and

Affan's new posters for the Kid Lit Quiz team were hanging up on the bulletin board across from the library. None of them were as nice as Jane's, but it didn't matter because the team was made. Jane had told him at practice on Friday. As he walked down the hallway, Tyson couldn't help thinking that things were really looking up.

CHAPTER 33

Jane

Stefan found me at lunch to say he couldn't make tomorrow's after-school practice. "Why not?" I asked.

"It's my science project. I need to test our controlled group of variables and—" I held up my hand.

"Never mind." Stefan would talk forever about his project if I let him. It was about sewage worms, which—don't even get me started. I wanted to enjoy my lunch.

"Now that there's an alternate, I didn't think you'd mind."

"You can still come to regionals though, right?"

"Yeah, I think so."

"You *think*?" I leveled my gaze at him.

Stefan took a deep breath. I could feel the bad news coming. "I'm not totally comfortable with our new teammate."

"Tyson, you mean? Or Hilman?"

"You know which one. Are you sure he didn't join as a joke? I didn't even know he could read, never mind liked it."

I frowned at Stefan's snarky comment. "You saw him on Friday. He got lots of the answers right."

"Yeah, but what's his motivation? He's not the typical Kid Lit Quiz–type kid."

"Meaning?"

"You know what I mean," Stefan said huffily. "If he joined as joke, he could ruin our chances at regionals."

I couldn't argue that Tyson's sudden interest in the team was surprising, but I also didn't want to turn away a teammate, especially one with potential. I thought back to the breakout kits we'd done in Mr. Lee's class. "We need Tyson," I said. "I'm not kicking him off."

Stefan shook his head at me. "If this turns into a disaster, don't say I didn't warn you." Stefan walked away. I sighed and packed up my lunch. Between sewage worms and his attitude, I'd lost my appetite.

After my conversation with Stefan, I went to the library, hoping to find a note from Y. There hadn't been anything since last week when I'd invited them to the Kid Lit Quiz team. I hoped I hadn't scared them away.

I breathed a sigh of relief when I opened *Liar & Spy*. A long note was waiting for me. It explained a lot, including the reason Y hadn't shown up. I reread the last paragraph. *What if you were hoping I'd be someone different?* What did Y mean by that?

"How did your practice go on Friday?" Mrs. Chin asked, startling me. I crumpled the note in my hand.

"It was great! Grandpa's a good coach. And we got another teammate!" I waited a beat and then told her who. "Tyson Flamand!"

"Really?" she said. Then caught herself. "Actually, I'm not surprised. He's been in here a lot lately. I guess he's discovered reading." She ran her finger along a row of books in the *L* section and pulled out one of Sienna's favorites, *Where the Mountain Meets the Moon* by Grace Lin. "His marks must have improved too, if he's on the team."

I frowned, not following. "What do you mean?"

"You know, because of the academic standards policy. Any student who wants to compete with a school team has to maintain a 65% average," she explained.

"65%?"

My stomach did a flip. I'd been at school with Tyson for long enough to know that that might be a problem. I thanked Mrs. Chin for letting me know and rushed out of the library. I couldn't lose our newest teammate this close to regionals.

With only a few minutes left in the lunch hour, I went to find Tyson. He was talking to Minju. At first, I thought he was telling her a story, but then he mentioned a smoke bomb and medi-pack. "Are you talking about a video game?" I interrupted.

Minju nodded. "*Mutant-Z*. Tyson's a total sweat."

"Does that mean you're good?" I asked.

"Lots of people are," Tyson said quickly. I was too distracted by Mrs. Chin's news to care about a video game, whatever it was called.

"I need to ask you a question." Minju took the hint and moved to her locker, which was a few spots down. "I just found out there's a rule that every kid on a team has to have 65% or higher in their classes to compete."

I didn't need to ask what his grades were like. The look on Tyson's face gave me the answer. I pushed aside my rising panic. "Can you check the Assignment

Tracker app on your phone?" The online system showed his up-to-date marks and what assignments he hadn't handed in.

"What's the point?" Tyson asked. "I know they aren't high enough."

"We need to figure out what we're going to do."

He looked at me with disbelief. "You still want me on the team?"

"We've come this far. I'm not letting a few percentage points stand in the way."

Not when I could do something about it.

CHAPTER 34

Tyson

The hundred-pound weight Tyson thought he'd lost a few hours ago had multiplied to a thousand.

He'd had no idea there was a rule about needing good grades to be on a school team. And now, as he swiped through the Assignment Tracker on his phone, he winced.

His highest mark was in English, but even it wasn't a sixty-five. The rest hovered around the mid-fifties. How was he supposed to get all his marks up to 65% before the tournament? He may as well give up now. "We can meet every day at lunch and after school on the days we don't have practice," Jane offered.

"Practice?" Minju asked. Tyson was sure she'd

heard the whole conversation. Strangely, he didn't care if Minju knew the truth about his grades, or Kid Lit Quiz.

"Regionals for Kid Lit Quiz," Jane told her.

Minju's eyebrows shot up. "I didn't know you were on the team."

"I won't be for long." Tyson slammed his locker closed harder than he needed to.

"If you need help, I can—"

Tyson shook his head at Minju. "It's a waste of time."

"You can't just give up," Jane said. Minju nodded in agreement.

"I can and I am." He shrugged with pretended indifference. There was no joke or prank that could get him out of this mess.

As he walked away, Jane called to him. "We'll meet in the library after school."

He didn't turn around and he wouldn't be going to the library. What was the point? He'd never be able to bump up his marks high enough to stay on the team. Jane's confidence in him only proved that she wasn't as smart as he'd thought she was.

Tyson had stewed about his marks, and how much work it would be to raise them, all afternoon. He felt guilty about letting Jane down. She'd been counting on him. But the situation was hopeless.

When the bell rang, he considered sneaking out a side door and heading home. His stomach sank at the idea of telling Ava he was off the team. She'd been so excited for him. She'd even made cue cards of information about the books she'd read to help him.

If he left school now, he'd never know if he could have stayed on the team. It'd be like his mom pulling the plug on Lizardo as he escaped the warehouse. He'd be pulling his own plug, sabotaging himself before he even tried.

When he got to the library, Jane was there and so was Minju. Their smiles told him he'd made the right choice.

"Minju says she'll help you with math and science. I can work with you on English and social studies. We'll make a list of the assignments you need to hand in."

Tyson opened Assignment Tracker and watched as Jane created a color-coded chart on the computer. His determination shriveled up like a raisin. There was no way he'd get all that done before the tournament.

"It's not as bad as it looks," Minju said, reading his mind.

After not caring about school work, or grades for the last few years, Tyson didn't know if he could do it. He wasn't like Max and Ava, or Minju and Jane. School was hard for him. He needed things explained more than once. Did *they* know how much work it was going to be?

Jane stared at him. She was fingering the silver heart pendant. "I wouldn't be here if I didn't think you could do it," she said.

Tyson looked between the girls. Despite everything in him screaming that it was pointless, Tyson found himself nodding. He wasn't ready to give up on the Kid Lit Quiz, or himself, just yet. "Okay, where do we start?"

CHAPTER 35

Jane

I didn't say anything about Tyson's grades to the rest of the team. Stefan had shown up for practice after all, and if he got wind that Tyson might not be allowed to compete, he'd have one more reason to quit.

"We're going to focus on the finals," Grandpa said after we'd done three practice rounds. "Just to make sure we're all on the same page." He chuckled at his pun and looked at Hilman and Tyson. "The points for each round get tabulated and then the three teams with the highest scores play in the final round. Clues are read out and players buzz in when they think they know the answer."

"But if you buzz in and answer wrong, your team

can't try again," Emily added, shaking her head. "That's what happened last year." Stefan's wrong answer had cost us the win. If he'd waited for another clue, we might have won.

Grandpa nodded and continued, "All the questions are related to a theme."

"At last year's regionals it was villains," I said.

"Another time it was fables," Emily added.

Hilman rubbed his tummy. He had a queasy look on his face. "Okay, first question!" Grandpa waved the card in the air.

"Wait," Tyson interrupted. "What's the theme?"

"Wizards!"

Hilman's stomach problems disappeared. He grinned in anticipation. Little did he know there were more wizards than just the ones at Hogwarts. Grandpa cleared his throat and began reading. "This wizard's original name was Olorin, but he's better known by a different name." We all looked at each other. Stefan leaned forward concentrating. "He's one of the few wizards on Middle Earth—"

"Gandalf!" Stefan said, pounding on the table.

"Yes!" Grandpa said.

Hilman got the answer to the next one, about Severus Snape. "Okay, final question. Ready?" He looked at all of us. Grandpa's eyes were sparkly. He drew out the pause making us grin with anticipation. "This old wizard dates back hundreds of years. He mentored a young boy named Wart, who became a great leader. He had an owl named Archimedes and changed young Wart into animals to teach him—"

This time, it was Tyson who slapped the table. "That's um…Oh, it's on the tip of my tongue!" He turned to me. "You know, *Sword in the Stone*! The Disney movie!"

"Merlin!" Kate shouted from the other side of the library.

"That's right, Katie." Grandpa laughed. "Merlin."

"You almost had it," I said to Tyson. But he shook his head, disappointed.

"*Almost* isn't going to get us to nationals," he muttered under his breath.

CHAPTER 36

Tyson

"I'll see all of you at the next practice," Coach Albert said as they left the library. From down the hallway, a group of guys burst out of the gym. The boys' basketball practice had just ended. Affan and Andrew were on that team. Tyson needed to make a quick getaway before he was spotted.

"Just a minute, everyone!" Coach Albert called. Tyson was tempted to ignore him and keep moving. "I almost forgot. You need this for regionals." Reluctantly, Tyson turned around. Coach Albert was giving out papers. "Permission forms since it's during the school day. Your parents need to sign them."

"Thanks," Tyson said. He held out his hand, but Coach Albert couldn't get the pages apart. He licked his fingers and rubbed the papers together. Tyson waited, his impatience mounting. How long until one of the boys noticed him?

Finally, Coach Albert got one permission form free and gave it to Tyson. "Thanks," Tyson said. He was almost at the door when he heard Affan call his name. His stomach clenched and he turned around.

"What are you doing here?" Affan asked coming over. Andrew trailed close behind. They were both sweaty from practice.

"I was just—" He wavered between the truth and making something up, but didn't get the chance. As soon as Coach Albert handed Stefan his permission form, Andrew grabbed it.

"'Kid Lit Quiz Regionals'?" Andrew read. "What is this?" He took in Jane, Emily, Stefan and Hilman, then zeroed in on Tyson. "Are you on this team?" Andrew stared at Tyson and burst into laughter. "With *them*?"

Jane looked between Tyson and Andrew, arching an eyebrow. "What does that mean?" she asked.

Andrew smirked. "You know, smart kids." He clamped a hand on Tyson's shoulder. "It's a joke, right? You're not actually on this team because you *want* to be?"

Tyson's cheeks flushed. He could feel the other kids, including Affan watching him, waiting for him to correct Andrew. If he admitted that he was, he'd never hear the end of it from his friends. If he said it was a joke his reputation would be saved, but he'd be the world's biggest jerk.

Tyson gulped. There was only one thing to do.

He grabbed Affan's glasses and put them on. Then he hiked up his pants and pressed his hair flat. "Nerds like us gotta stick together, right Hilman?" he asked in a nasally voice. Andrew and Affan laughed as he waddle-walked around them and spewed off a bunch of made-up facts. He looked at the Kid Lit Quiz team. No one had cracked a smile. Too late, Tyson realized his behavior wasn't funny to them. Not at all.

"Great recruit," Stefan said sarcastically. He grabbed the permission form back from Andrew and tossed it in the recycling bin. Then he stormed outside where his ride was waiting.

Stefan's reaction only made Andrew laugh harder. But Jane looked furious. Tyson's "joke" had just cost them a teammate.

Affan's phone buzzed with a text. "My mom's here." Tyson gave him back his glasses.

"Have fun with the Nerd Herd!" Andrew called as he and Affan left. When Tyson turned back to Coach

Albert, Jane, Emily, and Hilman, there was a moment of awkward silence.

"Are we a joke?" Hilman asked.

Tyson looked at his feet. "No."

He could feel Jane glaring at him. "Then why did you make it seem like we were?" Jane asked.

"Because he's embarrassed. Andrew and Affan consider us losers. He'll get teased for hanging out with us and for being on a team that is traditionally filled with nerds," Emily said matter-of-factly. "What's ironic is that the Kid Lit Quiz team has a better win-loss record than any sports team at Forest Hills. We, in fact, are the winners."

Jane picked Stefan's permission form out of the recycling bin. "Did you think you could hide that you were on the team?"

Tyson didn't answer.

"You need to tell your friends the truth. And you have to talk to Stefan. He already thought Kid Lit Quiz was a joke to you."

"It's not," Tyson said again.

"So prove it. Take something seriously for a change. Otherwise, you're the joke."

Jane's words rang in his ears all the way home.

There *was* more to him than being a prankster. He just had to find a way to let other people see it.

CHAPTER 37

Jane

I called Sienna as soon as I got home from Kid Lit Quiz practice and filled her in on everything. "I can't believe Tyson did that," she said when I told her how he'd acted.

"I know." I groaned. "He just wanted the laugh. I don't think he realized how rude he was being until after. Stefan stormed out, so who knows if he'll come back. I thought Hilman was going to cry. I told Tyson he has to apologize." I had no idea if he would, or if that would be enough to stop Stefan from quitting.

"What about the Undercover Book Club? Any notes from Y?"

I told her about Y's last note, how they'd explained

their reason for not joining the Kid Lit Quiz team. On the other end of the phone, Sienna sighed.

"How are things there?" Usually our conversations revolved around what was happening in my life. I winced, realizing that I hadn't asked her about the party she'd been to on Friday! She hadn't mentioned it either which was kind of weird. Had she decided not to go?

Sienna's voice faltered. "It's okay."

"What's wrong, Si?" I lay down on my bed and stared up at the ceiling. After all her upbeat phone calls, I thought Sienna was just having an off-day, but it turned out to be more than that.

"I've tried making friends. I'll literally smile at anyone. But it's different here. The girls are"—she broke off for a moment—"really, *really* interested in boys. The party last weekend wasn't what I expected. They played spin the bottle!" she whispered.

"What did you do?"

"I had to play!" she said, miserably. "I couldn't say no. And it landed on me and then I spun and it pointed to this boy named Vince." I held my breath waiting to hear the rest. "In front of everyone, I had to lean across the circle and kiss him!"

I cringed for her.

"Afterwards, he said he'd been hoping it would land on me."

"He likes you!"

"I know," she wailed. "But I don't want a boyfriend!"

"Just because he likes you doesn't mean you have to like him back. Anyway, no one can *force* you to be their girlfriend."

"All the other girls think it's so great." She was quiet for a minute. "At first, I played along, but now—ugh. Every conversation turns into one about our 'relationship.' It's so stupid," she continued. "They think I have all this experience with boys—"

"Why do they think that?" I asked.

There was a long pause. "Because…because I told them I had a boyfriend before I moved here." Sienna's confession came out a little strangled. "It was stupid—I know! Lindsay, my neighbor, asked the first day I met her. I lied and said yes. I wanted them to think I was like them and now it's all backfired. I've turned into someone I wouldn't want to be friends with." She let out a long sigh. "I wish I could just start over and be the real me."

The best part about Sienna was that I always felt like I could be myself with her. There wasn't much point in having a best friend if you had to pretend to be someone you weren't. "What's stopping you from starting over?" I asked. An idea started to form in my head. "Your Undercover Book Club idea worked for me—why don't you try it? There's got to be other kids there who like to read as much as you do."

There was silence on the other end of the phone. Maybe she thought it was a silly idea, or that it wouldn't work at her new school. Then she laughed with relief. "Oh my gosh! Jane! You're a genius!"

"Actually *you* are. It was your idea, remember?"

She giggled. "I can't believe I didn't think of it!"

I touched the heart pendant at my throat and pictured Sienna's face lighting up with excitement. A thousand miles might separate us, but it wasn't going to break us.

CHAPTER 38

Tyson

Tyson went to the library on Wednesday to check *Liar & Spy* for a reply to his note about why Y hadn't joined the Kid Lit Quiz.

Don't worry, she'd written. *I heard someone new joined and the team is really excited about it.* Tyson frowned. That probably wasn't true anymore. Not after yesterday's practice.

He wished he could explain things properly. Jane knew one part of him, but X knew the other part. Ava had been bugging him to reveal his identity. Maybe it was time. According to his sister, Jane was already his friend. All he had to do was be himself, like he was in his notes.

But the thought of showing himself made his stomach tighten. He wasn't the person she'd hoped Y would be. She wanted someone like Sienna.

Would she accept him as Y?

The thought consumed Tyson all afternoon. He wrote three versions of the same note when he should have been paying attention in social studies. Finally, he had a note ready to hide in the book. It explained that he wanted to meet. If she did too, he'd be waiting tomorrow at lunch in front of the library.

He glanced at the clock. Twenty-four hours from now, the secret would be out.

CHAPTER 39

Jane

Should we tell the girls?

I replayed Mom's question over and over in my head. She'd come home early and had been on the phone in her office. I hadn't meant to eavesdrop. I just needed more printer paper to make Kid Lit Quiz cue cards, so I opened the door a crack to make sure she wasn't on Zoom before I went in to get the paper.

She was standing at the window, looking outside and holding the phone to her ear. I was about to take a step inside when she said, "Should we tell the girls?"

I froze. Who was she talking to?

Mom let out a long sigh. "Okay. It's going to be

hard to keep this from them. You know Jane, she figures everything out."

It was Dad. It had to be. I gently shut the door and tiptoed away. What did she need to tell me? And why was it going to be hard to keep it a secret?

I ran through possibilities. The first one was that Dad had been hurt. But Mom didn't sound panicked, and she hadn't been acting differently. Could he be coming home early? I didn't think so because she'd have sounded more excited. There was one possibility that I didn't even want to think about—Dad's posting had been extended. That happened sometimes. He'd promised to be home before Day 1000, but the military might have other plans. What if instead of coming home in August, he was gone for the rest of the year?

"Everything okay?" Mom asked the next morning. "You're being really quiet."

"Just stressed about the tournament," I said. Which wasn't a total lie. I *was* worried. I'd been reading as much as possible. Mom had been quizzing me nightly from the online question bank. But *Should we tell the girls?* had bothered me all night. The fact that she was keeping it a secret made me worry even more.

As soon as I got to school, I checked *Liar & Spy*. I had a note in my backpack that I'd planned on leaving in the book, but when I read Y's, I realized I didn't have to. Y wanted to meet!

My stomach fluttered. I couldn't believe how nervous I was to meet someone I'd been writing to for weeks!

I tried not to think about it for the rest of the morning, but as the digital clock in Ms. Gill's room changed to 11:44, I realized in a few minutes I'd find out who Y was.

CHAPTER 40

Tyson

Over the past few days, Tyson hadn't had time to read. He'd been too busy pulling up his grades. So far his mark had gone up in social studies, thanks to the completed project on how to stop deforestation he'd handed in. He'd flunked it the first time after claiming that not printing it out *was* his project. Mr. Lee didn't find it as funny as the rest of the class.

Today, the pressure to complete his work had kept him from worrying about his meeting with Jane. But as the bell for lunch rang, Tyson's stomach was doing full-on cartwheels. He watched Jane pack up. Was she as nervous as he was?

She had mentioned in a letter that mysteries were her favorite books, and that she considered herself a good detective. Knowing that, Tyson wondered how she hadn't guessed he was Y. Minju had talked about *Mutant-Z* in front of Jane, and his printing must have looked familiar to her from the notes. But maybe he was the last person she suspected because he was right in front of her. Wasn't that how good mysteries went?

It was too late to worry about it now. Tyson watched the clock count down to the lunch hour. In a few minutes, the mystery of X and Y was going to be solved.

As soon as the bell rang, Tyson stood up and grabbed his books. He wanted to get to their meeting location first. Andrew moved in front of him, looking over his shoulder at Mr. Lee. Tyson knew that look. Andrew was planning something.

Affan was waiting for them by the door. Whatever it was, Tyson hoped it was quick. He didn't want to miss Jane.

"We're going to the gym," Andrew said.

"Do you have a practice?"

Andrew shook his head. "We don't. But Connor does."

Tyson frowned, not following. Andrew balled up his hands into fists. His mouth twisted into an angry sneer. "He was chirping at us about the game." During morning announcements, Mr. Morangi had mentioned the boys' basketball team had "lost a tough one," which was code for "got smoked" at yesterday's game. "All his stuff's in the locker room right now." Andrew smirked. "We're gonna put it where it belongs. In the toilet."

Tyson's first impulse was to laugh. It was hilarious to picture Connor looking for his Timberwolves jersey and then having to pull it out of the toilet soaking wet. Two weeks ago, the laughs would have made it totally worth doing...But things had changed.

Dumping Connor's stuff in the toilet might be funny to them, but it wouldn't be to Connor. Or to Mr. Morangi. "I don't know."

"We'll be in and out. No one will even notice," Andrew said quickly.

Tyson glanced at the clock. Convincing Andrew it was a bad idea was going to make him late. "I'll meet you there."

Andrew and Affan went one way, while Tyson went the other.

He got to the library, but there was no sign of Jane. Had he missed her?

He peeked into the library, wondering if she was waiting inside for him. Except for Mrs. Chin, it was empty. Where was she? He looked towards the office and spotted her. She was talking to Mrs. Hardy. Tyson took a deep breath. The weeks of keeping his identity a secret were about to be over.

CHAPTER 41

Jane

The bell for lunch hour rang. As I packed up my binder and pencil case, an announcement came over the PA system. "Jane McDonald, to the office, please. Jane McDonald." I didn't get called to the office very often, so it was weird to hear my name over the loudspeakers. Maybe I had a doctor's appointment that Mom had forgotten to tell me about? Or Kate was hurt and needed me?

When I walked into the office, Mrs. Hardy looked up from her computer, "Your mom's on her way to get you."

"Why?"

Mrs. Hardy cleared her throat and frowned. "She

said there was a family emergency and that you should be ready at the front doors. She said to pack up for the day."

"A family emergency?" I repeated. "Did she say anything else?"

Mrs. Hardy shook her head. "Sorry. That was all. You should hurry though. She said she was five minutes away."

A family emergency. If Mom was picking me up, she must be okay. Mrs. Hardy would have told me if something was wrong with Kate. That left Dad.

Should we tell the girls?

I burst out the office doors and almost ran into Tyson. "Hey, Jane," he said, grinning.

"I have to go!" I said, and dashed to my locker. I dumped my binders into my bag and slung it over my shoulder. What kind of emergency was important enough to make Mom leave work, and drag me out of school? And what about Kate? Why wasn't Mom picking her up too? I was already waiting at the front of the school when Mom pulled up. It wasn't until I got into the front seat and slammed the door shut that I remembered I was supposed to meet Y.

My heart sank. Were they still there, waiting around for me?

What would they think when X never showed? The question was quickly pushed out of my head I saw Mom's expression.

"Is it Dad?" I asked.

"Dad? No, he's fine."

I breathed a sigh of relief. "Then what's the family emergency?"

"It's Grandpa."

A tingly feeling spread up from the base of my neck.

"He wasn't feeling well, so Grandma took him to the hospital. While they were waiting to see the doctor, he collapsed."

I waited for Mom to say more. "But he's okay, right?"

Mom shook her head. She bit her lip to keep her chin from trembling. "He had a massive stroke. Right there. Grandma was beside him, but there was nothing she could do." A hot flush of tears started behind my eyes.

"Grandpa? Is he—is he—" I couldn't say it. I couldn't even think it.

"He's breathing," Mom said. "But unconscious. They don't know if he'll make it." Her voice caught.

"Mom." My voice broke. It was a question and a wail at the same time. Her arms were around me. Her shoulder soaked up my tears.

CHAPTER 42

Tyson

Tyson stood frozen in place. Whatever he'd been expecting, it wasn't that.

He'd thought Jane would be shocked. Surprised that she hadn't figured it out. Maybe a little disappointed that it was him.

But he didn't think she'd run away. He'd been planning on hanging out in the library with Jane for the lunch hour, laughing at all the clues she'd missed. He even had a final note for her in his pocket. It said all the things he worried he wouldn't be able to.

A whistle pierced the air. Andrew was the only kid he knew who could make that noise. He and Affan were waiting for him down the hall, outside of the gym doors. He didn't want to prank Connor, but couldn't think of an excuse that would get him out of it.

The boys slid into the gym one by one. The coach was talking to the team on the far court.

They paused before going into the boys' change-room, making sure no one saw them. "This is his stuff right here," Andrew said, pointing to the jersey hanging off a hook. "What about his shoes?" He grabbed one off the shelf.

A jersey in a toilet was one thing, but high-end sneakers like Connor's would take forever to dry. Plus, would he ever want to wear them again?

They froze when a toilet flushed.

Connor stepped out of the cubicle. He looked as surprised to see them as they were to see him. "What are you doing?" he asked. "Why are you holding my shoe?" He eyed Andrew suspiciously.

Affan gave a nervous laugh. Tyson had to think fast or this prank was going to end badly.

"We were leaving something. For you," Tyson said. "Well, I was."

"Oh yeah? What?"

Tyson racked his brain. What did he have that would make sense? He put his hand in his pocket and felt the folded-up letter he'd written to Jane. "An apology. My mom said I had to write you a letter for what we did to your jersey. And the hat. I was going to leave it in your shoe. So you'd find it later."

Connor's expression was still skeptical.

"I have it right here," he said and pulled it out. "It's kind of embarrassing," he said.

Andrew smirked. "I'd like to hear it."

"Me too," agreed Affan.

Tyson swore at them under his breath, and began reading, well, ad libbing, the letter. "Dear Connor, I'm really sorry for disrespecting the Timberwolves. I know you like them and just because they aren't the best team doesn't mean you should give up on them." The next words came surprisingly easy. "I've recently started reading more and trying harder at school. I even joined the Kid Lit Quiz team, but didn't tell anyone." He looked at his friends. "The other day, Andrew and Affan saw me with the team. I was embarrassed and tried to make a joke about it. But it's not a joke. And neither are the Timberwolves. Sorry for not taking what you care about seriously. Sincerely, Tyson."

He folded the note and put it back in his pocket. No one spoke for a minute. For the first time in maybe ever, Tyson didn't want a laugh from his friends. "We won't touch your stuff anymore," Tyson promised.

"Yeah, right," Connor said.

"No, really. I promise."

Affan and Andrew shifted uncomfortably. "Me too," said Affan.

With a reluctant sigh, Andrew nodded. "Same here."

Connor's expression relaxed. He held his fist up for a bump. Tyson bumped it back. The tension in the air disappeared. "I better get back to practice. Coach'll wonder what's going on," Connor said.

As soon as the door shut after him, Andrew looked at Tyson. "Is that for real?"

"What? The note?"

"What you said about wanting to be on that team?"

Tyson nodded. "Yeah. Except I'm probably going to get kicked off because of my grades."

"It's all about book trivia, right?" Affan asked. Tyson nodded. "My brother was on a team at his school. I had to go to one of his competitions. It was actually cooler than I thought it'd be."

"So, you're like a nerd now," Andrew said, but not in a mean way. He shook his head in disbelief. Tyson laughed. It reminded him of that moment in *Holes* when Zero and Stanley surprised everyone and people started to see them for who they really were.

CHAPTER 43

Jane

"This way," Mom said when we got to the hospital. Everything was a blur as we raced down the halls from the parking garage to Grandpa's room.

Finally, I saw Grandma sitting on a chair in the hallway and my heart gave a leap. She stood up when she saw us and I threw my arms around her. "How are you?" Mom asked.

"I'm okay. The doctors are with him."

"What happened?" Mom asked.

Grandma took a breath. She was rattled and as she explained, I could see why. "We were with his doctor and all of a sudden what he was saying didn't make sense. Part of his face froze." Grandma looked at Mom, her eyes wide and scared. "The doctor started shouting for help and then there were all these people around him. They took him away and I didn't know where he was. Finally, someone came back to get me and that's when they told me—" She broke off. Her hands shook as she brought them to her face.

"Shh, shh. It's okay. It's okay," Mom said.

A doctor came out of the room. He had a serious expression, but a kind face. "I'm Dr. Sharma," he said to Grandma and Mom. "You're Albert's wife and daughter?" He confirmed. They nodded. "Come in. He's not conscious, but you can see him."

It was dark in the room; the curtains were drawn over the windows. I was afraid to look at Grandpa at first. All the tubes and beeping machines scared me. How could that be my grandpa lying there? He looked so old and weak.

Grandma went right up to the bed and took his hand in hers. "Albert," she breathed.

"We're waiting to get the test results back," Dr. Sharma said.

"And then what?" Mom asked. She was staring at Grandpa, frowning.

Dr. Sharma met her eyes. "It was a massive stroke. He was lucky it happened at the hospital. If he'd been anywhere else—" He shook his head at what that reality would have been.

Mom kept pressing Dr. Sharma for more answers. "I need to understand what the options are. If his brain activity is low—"

"We won't know until the tests come back—"

"I know that, but is it possible he could wake up?"

"It's possible."

"But not probable."

Dr. Sharma gave her a stern look. "I didn't say that."

"I'm just trying to make sense of this," Mom replied tersely.

"Julie." Grandma's voice was sharp. Mom took a breath and nodded.

"I'll be back as soon as I know anything," Dr. Sharma said gently, and left the room. The three of us surrounded Grandpa's bed.

"Can he hear us?" I whispered to Mom.

She was staring at him. "Maybe. It depends how badly the stroke affected his brain function." I waited for her to say more. To tell me it would be all right. "We have to be prepared. If the tests come back and there's no brain activity, the Grandpa we know is already gone."

My chest got tight as I realized why she'd picked

me up from school. She knew how close I was to him. This might be my last chance to say goodbye to him.

I pressed myself against Mom. Her arms went around my shoulders and I grabbed her around the waist. Grandma held Grandpa's hand to her cheek and put it to her lips. "What will I do without you?" she whispered.

I held my breath waiting for Grandpa to say something, a mumble, a nod, anything. But he stayed frozen in place. A machine connected to his nose and mouth helped him breathe.

Grandma sat down in a chair but didn't let go of Grandpa's hand. Mom and I sat across from her. None of us spoke for a long time. It wasn't until Mom left the room to call a neighbor to pick Kate up from school that I realized I'd just be getting dismissed now.

I didn't want to intrude on Grandma, but she beckoned me over. "Come and sit with me." She patted the chair beside her. "Or sit on the bed and hold his hand." The one with the tube sticking out of it? What if it popped out?

"You won't hurt him," Grandma said. She was being strong, despite Grandpa lying there.

"It doesn't look like him," I said. I put a finger gingerly on his hand, running it along his dry skin.

"He's going to wake up. I know it," she said.

What would happen if he didn't wake up? Beeping monitors and the hiss of the machines filled the quiet room.

There was a knock on the door and Dr. Sharma walked in with Mom. She gave me a weak smile. "I've got results from the MRI," said the doctor.

I tried to read his expression, but it gave nothing away. Mom's eyes darted to Grandma and to me.

"The damage isn't severe. Your husband's brain functions are all normal, except for some damage in one region, which isn't serious, so there's no reason he won't be able to resume normal activities."

Mom, Grandma and I hugged and wiped tears of relief from our eyes. Grandpa was going to be okay!

"When will he wake up?" Grandma asked.

For that, Dr. Sharma had no answer. "Comas are a body's way of healing. We can take him off the ventilator but there's no way to predict how long he'll stay unconscious. It could be hours, or it could be days."

"What if he has another one?" I asked in a small voice.

"He'll be on blood thinners to prevent another clot. That doesn't mean it's impossible, but it's unlikely." Dr. Sharma turned to Grandma, "Your husband was lucky.

He was in the right place when this happened. A nurse will be in to take out the breathing tube and then we'll just have to wait and see."

"Get down here and give me a hug!" Grandma said to Dr. Sharma. He bent down and she planted a red lipstick kiss on his cheek.

After Dr. Sharma left, Mom offered to take Grandma and me to get something to eat. "I don't want to leave him," Grandma said.

"You go, Grandma. I'll stay," I offered.

Mom gave me a grateful smile. "Come on, Mom. You need to keep your strength up."

Grandma looked at Grandpa doubtfully. "What if he needs me?"

"I'll be right here. I promise."

"Hold his hand, Jane. So he knows he's not alone," Grandma said. "Do you have a book? You could read to him."

The only book I had was the last suggestion Y had given me. I went to my backpack and pulled it out. "I could read this to him," I said and held up *Hello, Universe.*

"He'd like that," Grandma said.

Normally, I wouldn't have thought twice about being in the same room as Grandpa, but as the door closed after Grandma and Mom, I got anxious. What if something happened? I looked for the button to buzz the nurse. It was within arm's reach. So was Grandpa's hand. I moved the chair closer to the bed and tucked my fingers under his. With my other hand, I opened the book.

Forcing myself to focus on what mattered right now, Grandpa, I opened the book and started reading.

The book had some funny parts and every time I read a line that made me smile, I peeked at him, just in case he'd heard it and was laughing too.

"Grandpa," I whispered. "You might not be able to hear me, but I want you to know I love you more than anything. Even more than reading—and you know how much I love books."

At the mention of books, I remembered Y and how I'd left them, whoever they were, waiting.

I slumped in the chair thinking that I'd probably just missed them when I rushed out of the office. Tyson had been standing there. He might've seen Y. And then, I got a funny thought. What if Y had thought Tyson was X? He was standing just where we'd planned to meet.

That would have been a classic case of an identity mix-up.

CHAPTER 44

Tyson

When Mr. Lee took afternoon attendance, Jane's seat was empty, which got Tyson thinking: maybe finding out he was Y hadn't been the reason she'd raced away. A Kid Lit Quiz practice was scheduled for after school, so Tyson headed to the library when the dismissal bell rang. When he got there, Mrs. Chin was standing in front of Stefan, Emily, and Hilman. There was no sign of Jane, or Coach Albert.

"I've got some bad news," Mrs. Chin said. "Jane's grandpa is in the hospital."

Tyson stared at Mrs. Chin. "Is he going to be okay?"

"I'm not sure. Jane's mom called the school to let us know, but we haven't heard anything else."

"Will he be better by the tournament?" asked Hilman.

Mrs. Chin shook her head. "I don't think so." She looked at them sadly. She turned to her desk where two students were waiting to sign out books.

"So what happens now? Do we find another coach? When will Jane be back at school?" Hilman asked. All of these questions were on Tyson's mind too.

"If Jane can't be there, there's no point in competing," Emily said in her usual matter-of-fact tone.

After all Jane had done to keep the team together, Tyson couldn't believe what he was hearing. "No way! We have to compete. We're a team."

Stefan shot Tyson a look. "Are we? I thought we were a joke."

Tyson was about to apologize when Emily picked up her bag and started for the door. "Where are you going?" Tyson asked.

"Home. We have no coach and we're missing our best player. What's the point in practicing? We're not going to win."

"I'm with Emily," said Stefan. "The science fair is coming up. I need to focus my energy on something I might actually do well in."

Tyson shook his head at them. "You're both bailing?

Seriously?" He slouched in his chair. "Some teammates you are." Neither of them looked back.

Hilman turned to Tyson. "Guess it's just us." His legs didn't quite reach the floor as he swung them back and forth.

Tyson had never been to a Kid Lit Quiz tournament, but he knew two players and no coach wasn't going to cut it. He had to figure out a way to save the team. He wasn't doing it just for himself. He was doing it for Jane.

"Half a team is better than no team," he said to Hilman with as much enthusiasm as he could muster. Tyson went to one of the library's computers and pulled up the Kid Lit Quiz online question bank. He turned to Hilman who was ready with a notebook and pencil. Until they found someone else, Tyson would have to be coach and player. "Question number one…"

CHAPTER 45

Jane

It was Sunday and Grandpa was still in a coma. Between me, Mom, and Grandma, he was never alone. When it was my turn, I read to him. We were halfway through *Hello, Universe* already. Y had made another good pick.

"Hi," Mom said as she came into the room. "How's he doing?" she asked, pulling up a chair beside me.

"The same."

"I have a surprise for you," Mom said.

I looked at her. She was smiling, which seemed out of place in the hospital room. As the days dragged on, I'd been wondering if Grandpa was ever going to come out of the coma. "What is it?"

"Go look in the hallway."

I put the book face down on the chair and opened the door. Compared to the dim lights in Grandpa's room, the fluorescent lights were blinding. I looked up and down the hallway.

"Psst."

Someone was around the corner. I followed the sound.

A man in camouflage was pressed against the wall. "Dad!" I screamed.

"Janey!" He opened his arms and I ran into them. Dad picked me up and swung me around.

"You're back!" I was laughing and crying at the same time.

"I'm on compassionate leave," he corrected. "It took some work to get it approved, but I'm here."

I hugged Dad so tightly he pretended to gasp for breath. I didn't want to let go. I tilted my head up to look at him. He was tanned from the Middle Eastern sun. The hair around his temples was grayer. "How long will you be home?" I asked, and then regretted the question. Whatever he said, it wouldn't be long enough.

"A week," he said.

My chest tightened at how fast the time would go, and also the reason that had brought him back.

I buried my face in his uniform and breathed in the smell of him.

"I'm so glad you're home," I whispered.

"Me too, honey," he said, and gave me an extra-long Dad squeeze.

CHAPTER 46

Tyson

Tyson made an X over the last assignment on Jane's color-coded chart. He couldn't believe it! He'd finished everything! He hadn't done it alone; his whole family had helped, even Max. Minju had come over on Saturday to work on math. Tyson had done more homework in the last week than in his whole life put together. He still didn't know if it would be enough, but at least he'd tried.

The next day, he went to each teacher, showing them what he'd done. Ms. Gill shook her head in amazement. She checked each assignment. They weren't all correct; he wasn't Einstein, but as she entered the grades into the Assignment Tracker, he watched his mark go up. And up. And up.

When she was done a 67% showed on his screen.

It was the same in the other classes too. With the help of his friends and family, Tyson had done it. And best of all, he'd proved to himself that he could do it. Unfortunately, the person he most wanted to tell still wasn't at school.

Jane had been away from school for six days when Tyson stopped in the library. He had a note for her. It was the one he'd wanted to give her last week. The same one that had been his pretend apology to Connor. It said all the things he had worried he'd be too nervous to say in person if they'd met that day as planned. Mrs. Chin looked up when he entered the library and smiled.

He went directly to *Liar & Spy* and placed the note between its pages, along with a list of recommended books, just in case Jane decided to check.

Mrs. Hardy had followed Tyson in and stopped at Mrs. Chin's desk. "Jane McDonald's dad just called. He's coming by later to collect homework and asked if you could put together some books for her."

Tyson stopped in his tracks to listen to the rest of the conversation. "How's her grandpa?" Mrs. Chin asked.

"He didn't say," said Mrs. Hardy.

Mrs. Chin sighed and shook her head. "I'll pull a few books for her, but she's read half of the library."

A swell rose in Tyson's chest. He could help! He had a whole list of recommendations ready.

"*The Barren Grounds* by David A. Robertson," he blurted. It was the first title that came to him. "Or *City Spies* by James Ponti. Jane loves mysteries."

Mrs. Chin looked at him curiously. "What other books do you recommend?"

There'd been one about pajamas and another with a fox on the cover. He went back to *Liar & Spy* and pulled the list out. "All these ones," he said handing it to her.

"What is going on?" Mrs. Chin shook her head. "Why are you leaving notes in books?"

"It's kind of a long story."

Mrs. Chin scanned the list and smiled. "These are all very good choices. How do you know Jane would like them?"

"Because we're in a secret book club. Jane called it the Undercover Book Club. She left a note a while ago in this book." Tyson pulled *Liar & Spy* off the shelf. "I found the note and then I read the book. She asked for a suggestion, so I gave her one Mr. Nucci read last year. We went back and forth like that." The last book she'd suggested was *Amari and the Night Brothers* by B. B. Alston.

Mrs. Chin's mouth hung open and Tyson bit back a smile. Finally, she sputtered, "Which books did you recommend?"

Tyson had to think. "*Harbor Me*, then *Holes* and *The Book Thief. Hello, Universe* was my last suggestion."

"And you read the books Jane recommended to you?"

"Yeah. I'm still working on *Bloom*. We kept our identities a secret, but I figured out it was Jane."

"Well." Mrs. Chin pulled herself together and turned her attention back to the list of books Tyson had given her. "I think Jane would like all these suggestions. I wonder if you'd like to put a note in with them, so she knows they came from you."

Tyson went to *Liar & Spy* and took out the note he'd left. He gave it to Mrs. Chin. In it was everything he wanted to say.

CHAPTER 47

Jane

I'd been reading about people in comas and how important talking to them was, so even if Grandpa didn't look like he could hear me, I wanted him to know I was here. As long as Mom and Dad let me stay by his side, I talked and read out loud to him.

Mom had tried to convince me to go to school, but there was no point. I wouldn't have been able to concentrate anyway. My teachers put together a week's worth of assignments and I worked on them at Grandpa's bedside. Mrs. Chin had sent me a bag of books too. I'd made a game of reaching in and picking one without looking. I had just finished *The Barren Grounds*, a book that reminded me of *The Lion, the Witch and the*

Wardrobe, when I grabbed *When You Reach Me*. It was by Rebecca Stead, who'd written *Liar & Spy*. I'd read the book before—a few times. Seeing its familiar cover made me feel like an old friend had returned.

At the bottom of the bag was a note. I recognized the printing. It was from Y.

> Dear Jane,
> Surprise! It's me, Tyson, aka Y!
>   I just wanted to say thank you for helping me. Not just with school stuff. With other stuff too. I think you know what I'm talking about. The Undercover Book Club is about more than reading. A lot more.
>
>   See ya,
>
>   Tyson

A P.S. was scribbled in a different color at the bottom.

>   I'm sorry your grandpa's in the hospital. I heard that reading to people who are in comas can help. Mrs. Chin let me pick out a bunch of books for you. I hope you like them.

"It was Tyson!" I laughed with surprise. "I can't believe I didn't figure it out! Some detective I am!" I'd gotten better at one-sided conversations. It even felt like Grandpa was listening sometimes. Being at the hospital for the last few days made me feel like I was in a bubble. I'd called Sienna once to tell her what had happened, but it had been a short conversation.

I sat back in my chair and let things sink in. "Right about now we'd be having our Kid Lit Quiz practice to get ready for the regionals."

Looking at Grandpa lying in his hospital bed, I knew that even though it meant kissing my chances of going to nationals, and seeing Sienna, goodbye, I couldn't compete. How could I concentrate with Grandpa in a coma?

I was so lost in my thoughts that when Grandpa's hand jerked, I thought I'd imagined it. I stared at him waiting for it to happen again. His eyelids fluttered. They had! I saw them. "Nurse! Somebody!" I yelled. I fumbled with the call button and pressed it. "Somebody, get in here!" I stood right beside Grandpa's bed and leaned over him. "Grandpa? Grandpa? It's me, it's Jane!"

A low moan came from his lips. I was shaking. It was happening. "He's waking up!" I said to the nurse who rushed in. She grabbed his other hand. "Albert? Can you hear me? Squeeze my hand if you can."

We waited. I barely took a breath and then I felt it, weak at first and then stronger. His fingers closed around mine. "Grandpa!" I cried.

And then he went slack. His fingers loosened and the machine above his bed that tracked his heartbeat flatlined.

The nurse's eyes flew from the machine to Grandpa and she pressed a buzzer on the wall. "Code Blue!" Suddenly, the room was filled with nurses and doctors and I was pushed aside, my bag of books kicked under the bed.

"He was waking up," I cried. "What happened?"

No one answered. They were too busy trying to give my grandpa back his life.

CHAPTER 48

Tyson

"This is a waste of time," Stefan huffed. Tyson had called an emergency meeting of the Kid Lit Quiz team in the library. "We can't compete at regionals. We don't have a coach! And you and Hilman have never competed before. We'll embarrass ourselves."

"We have a coach. Mr. Morangi agreed to fill in for the tournament. And, I found another teammate," Tyson told them, proudly.

As if on cue, the library doors opened and Minju breezed in. "Sorry I'm late," she said, taking a seat beside Tyson.

"You're the new teammate?" Stefan asked. "Approved by who? You? The guy who thinks everything's a joke? Sorry if I'm not super confident in our chances when you're leading the team."

Tyson had been excited when Minju offered to fill in for Jane, but listening to Stefan made him wonder if the whole thing was a mistake. Even though Tyson had apologized to the team for his un-funny joking, Stefan didn't seem ready to forgive him anytime soon. Or ever.

"Actually, Stefan, Tyson's the only one taking this seriously. He's worked his butt off to make sure we can go to regionals. He's kept this team going, which is more than I can say for you." Minju arched an eyebrow, daring Stefan to respond.

Stefan glared back, but kept his mouth shut.

"We have to give regionals a shot, even without Jane and Coach Albert."

"He's right," Emily piped up. Tyson threw her a grateful smile. "Not you, Tyson. I meant Stefan. We'll most likely lose."

Tyson knew that. But he still wanted to try. What was that phrase of Minju's? You miss 100% of the shots you don't take? He was tired of sitting on the sidelines. It was time to get in the game.

"I thought we could go over some practice questions. Ready?" he asked. Hilman, Emily, and Minju got out paper and pens. Reluctantly, Stefan did too. "Question one," Tyson read. Through the library window, Mr. Morangi was watching them. A look of pride on his face. Tyson turned back to the sheet in his hand. "At what fictional school will you find…"

CHAPTER 49

Jane

Grandpa was gone.

I had to face the fact that it was possible. Mom and Grandma sat on either side of me. We'd been staring at the wall, clutching each other's hands in silence for the last hour.

Mom's phone rang. "Hi," she answered in a monotone. I could hear Dad's tinny voice asking if there was an update. "Not yet. I'll let you know as soon as we hear anything." Then he put Kate on. Mom forced a smile. "Hi, sweetie! The doctors are with Grandpa right now. As soon as he's better, you can come and see him."

I looked at Mom. Should she be filling Kate's head with things that might not happen? As if reading my mind, Mom said, "We have to think positive. He's going to make it."

"Yes, of course he is," Grandma piped up. "Because if he doesn't, I'll kill him."

It was good to hear Grandma's feisty words and for a minute my spirits lifted. The door to Grandpa's room opened and Dr. Sharma appeared. He cleared his throat. Before he could even start speaking, Grandma broke into tears.

Because Dr. Sharma had smiled. A big, toothy grin that made the apples of his cheeks puff out. "He's stable. And, he's awake!"

Mom grabbed me so hard that my shoulder crunched against her. We laughed and hugged and cried.

"You can see him if you like, one at a time though. He's been through a lot, but he's a fighter."

I closed my eyes and let out a long sigh of relief. *Grandpa was going to be okay.*

"Janey," Grandpa's voice was weak, scratchy and dry. I was even more afraid to go near him now than I had been when he was first in the coma.

He shut his eyes. "I'm tired," he said.

Grandma and Mom had gone in first. The lights

were dim in his room. We were only allowed short visits because he needed to rest.

"Reading" Grandpa whispered. "Thank you."

"You could hear me?"

A slight nod.

"I love you, Grandpa." My voice was choked, thick with tears.

"Me too." He raised his hand slowly and I grabbed for it. I stayed beside him until his breathing turned deep and even.

"Is he asleep?" Mom said coming into the room. I nodded. She came around to stand with me and we both watched him.

"I never thought watching someone sleep would be such a relief."

Mom gave a little laugh. "I know. Well, Dr. Sharma is confident he's out of the woods so we should take Grandma home now. She's exhausted. And tomorrow I'll bring Kate to see him."

Sienna had been texting me nonstop looking for updates. Finally, I could share some good news.

Since I'd barely slept for almost a week, Mom and Dad let me miss school again the next day. We spent the morning resting at home and then went to the hospital together in the afternoon. Since Grandpa's condition had been changed to "stable," he was allowed up to four visitors at a time.

The only thing better than hearing Grandpa's laughter was having Dad home.

"I don't want you to leave again," I said as he was tucking me in to bed that evening.

"It'll just be for a couple more months," he said. "And then—" He paused. I held my breath. "And then, there's going to be some changes."

Should we tell the girls? echoed in my head. I'd forgotten about it until now. "What changes?" I asked.

He smiled. "I don't want to be away from you and Kate and Mom anymore. It's too hard. We weren't going to tell you until it was finalized, but I'm retiring from the army."

"You are?" He'd been in the army since he was eighteen.

He nodded. "I've been with the military for twenty-seven years. I've had a good career."

"So after this posting you'll be back with us for good?" It sounded too perfect to be true.

"That's the plan."

I held Dad's hand, wishing he could retire this

minute so I wouldn't have to say goodbye to him again. "It's just a few more months, Janey," he whispered.

"Can you stay until I fall asleep?" I asked. It was sort of babyish, but I didn't care. I needed to hang on to the feeling of having him with me until he came home for good.

CHAPTER 50

Tyson

Tyson, Emily, and Minju walked into a huge room filled with excited kids. "There must be 500 people here!" Minju said in awe. The main floor of a convention hall had been set up with tables and chairs. A banner across the stage read: *Super Book Invitational: Kid Lit Quiz Regional Championship*. A golden trophy shone underneath it. A large timer on the stage was counting down the minutes until the tournament started.

A man wearing a top hat and tails walked around the tables, greeting the kids. "That's the Quizineer," Emily said.

Mr. Morangi was waiting at the front doors for Stefan. Hilman had arrived moments after Tyson's parents dropped off him and Minju. They were coming back in a couple of hours to watch the finals. "We might not even make it," Tyson had warned them. And now that he saw how many other kids were competing, his hopes sank.

"Who're they?" Minju asked Emily. A team walked through the crowd, high-fiving other kids as they passed.

"Whyte Ridge Middle School." Emily groaned. "Last year's winner." Even if no one had told Tyson they were the regional champions, he'd have guessed. They walked with an air of confidence none of the other teams had.

Hilman rubbed his tummy. He had a pained look on his face. "I have to use the restroom," he said, and raced away.

Minju looked at Tyson. "Is he always like that?"

"He says it's a nervous stomach," Emily answered. "But it could be an undiagnosed dietary sensitivity."

Tyson rubbed his stomach. He felt a little queasy too.

"Forest Hills School," Tyson said to the woman at the registration table. She put a checkmark on the list but didn't give them the special badges the other kids had.

"Your whole team has to be with you, including your coach, before you can go to your assigned seats.

You can wait over there." She pointed to an area where other kids stood in groups of two or three.

Tyson nodded and stepped to the side. The team behind him were dressed as fairy-tale characters. Tyson ran through their character names as a quick reminder of which was which.

"Stefan isn't usually late," Emily said. They were jostled as a group of three mice walked by, followed by the farmer's wife.

"Maybe there was traffic?" Minju wondered out loud.

Tyson had a different thought. Stefan had stayed for practice the other day, but had grumbled the whole time. "He's still mad at me. Do you think…" He let his voice trail off. Would Stefan sabotage the whole team just to make a point to Tyson?

Mr. Morangi gave them the answer a moment later. "I've got bad news," he said. "Stefan isn't coming. His mom just called."

"Why not?" Emily asked.

"There was a problem with his science project. All his samples were destroyed. It sounds like he had to redo all his testing."

Emily hit her palm to her forehead. "Not the sewage worms?"

Mr. Morangi nodded. "Unfortunately, his dog got curious."

There was a round of "Ewwww!"

Tyson let out a shaky breath. He was relieved that he wasn't the reason Stefan hadn't showed, but that still left them a player short. "I guess Hilman will have to play," Tyson said.

"Where is he?" Mr. Morangi asked.

"Restroom," they all said together. The timer on the stage was down to ten minutes. Most of the teams, including Whyte Ridge, had taken their assigned spots at the tables. He was starting to panic. After all his work to get here, Tyson didn't want to go home without competing.

He also didn't want to let Jane down. He looked toward the entrance, hoping for some kind of miracle. Then a group of grown-ups by the doors moved out of the way and someone waved to him.

His face split into a grin and he waved back. "I knew she wouldn't miss this!"

CHAPTER 51

Jane

When I woke up the next morning, Dad was in the kitchen wearing Grandma's apron and frying up a big breakfast of bacon and eggs. Mom was at the counter with her laptop. "Morning, sleepyhead," Dad said, kissing me on the cheek.

"Are you going to work?" I asked.

She shook her head. "I'll get caught up this morning and then take the afternoon off." She smiled at Dad.

"I don't even know what day it is," I said with a groan.

"TGIF," Dad answered.

Friday!

I gasped. "Regionals! They're today!" I looked at the clock. "In an hour!" Worrying about Grandpa and practically living at the hospital for a week had kept me out of the loop about the Kid Lit Quiz team. If there even was a team anymore. We didn't have a coach and I didn't know if Tyson's marks were high enough for Mr. Morangi to let him compete. "What should I do?" I wailed. It was a thirty-minute drive to the convention center.

My parents sprang into action. "I'll call the school and make sure the other kids are going. You," she pointed at me. "Go shower!"

"I'll pack lunch," Dad said. All I could do was cross my fingers that the rest of my team was on their way.

I'd never been this nervous walking into a tournament before. Sienna had always been by my side. I led Dad up the stairs to the convention center ballroom. He'd found a parking spot right outside, but I was still cutting it close. The tournament started in less than ten minutes! "All these kids are competing?" he asked looking around. Lots were in costumes. I got a twinge remembering how much fun Ms. Krauss had had deciding on our "team look."

I looked for my team. I'd tried texting Emily, but got no reply.

With so many kids milling around, it was hard to get a clear view of the space. I saw the Quizineer making his rounds, and then the Whyte Ridge team. I couldn't help but scowl at them. And then, across the floor, I saw a familiar face.

CHAPTER 52

Tyson

"You made it!" Tyson said, grinning. Minju pulled Jane into a hug.

"You're late," Emily said. But then she smiled too.

"This is my dad," Jane said, introducing him to Mr. Morangi.

As Jane's dad explained the events of the past few days to their principal, Jane pulled the team aside. "Okay," she said. "This is it. Is Hilman here?"

"Restroom," Emily said.

"Well, we have a team of four, plus a spare. Is Mr. Morangi the coach?"

Tyson nodded. The clock onstage was in the last five minutes of the countdown. The four kids and Mr. Morangi went over to the registration desk. "Forest Hills School," Jane said.

"Write your names here." The man turned his clipboard toward the kids. He was wearing a curly, blue-haired wig and a red shirt that said *Thing One*. Jane, Tyson, Minju, and Emily each wrote their names in the blank spaces, then passed the clipboard to Mr. Morangi.

Just as he took the pen, a voice called out, "Wait!"

Jane let out a squeal of delight. A woman with brown hair and glasses ran up to them. A colorful scarf trailed behind her. She pulled Jane into a hug and gave the other kids a big grin.

"Ms. Krauss!"

"I heard what happened to your grandpa," she said to Jane. "I'm so sorry."

"How did you find out?" Jane asked.

"Sienna sent me an email."

Tears sprang to Jane's eyes. "She did?"

Ms. Krauss nodded. "I talked to Mr. Morangi yesterday, but wasn't sure I could book off a personal day at such short notice. It got approved an hour ago and I raced down here. I couldn't miss it!"

Mr. Morangi handed the pen to Ms. Krauss. She signed her name with a flourish. "Tyson, right?" she asked, turning to him. "Mr. Morangi told me how hard you worked to get here. I'm really impressed."

Tyson didn't bother trying to hide his smile anymore. *So this is what it feels like,* he thought. To have all these people proud of him just made him want to try harder and do better.

"We're at table ten," Emily said. "We have three minutes to get ready."

Minju grabbed Jane's hand and gave it an excited squeeze. "Oh my gosh! I didn't think this would be so nerve-racking!"

"What about Hilman?" Tyson asked. "Should someone go check on him?" Tyson understood how he felt. Seeing hundreds of kids ready to for a book trivia battle was more intimidating than he'd imagined.

Mr. Morangi volunteered to check on Hilman, and Ms. Krauss pointed out the alternate player section in the stands. Hilman wouldn't get to play now that everyone was here, but that didn't mean he wasn't part of the team.

Table ten was halfway between the door and the stage and as the timer ticked down to the final minute, the Forest Hills Kid Lit Quiz team took their seats.

CHAPTER 53

Jane

Nothing could have prepared me for seeing Ms. Krauss. And to know that she was here because of Sienna completely lifted my spirits. She gave us a thumbs-up when she sat down.

"Welcome to Kid Lit Quiz regionals!" the Quizineer began. Everyone cheered. He walked around the stage with his microphone and the crowd quieted. He went over the rules and then announced that due to a generous donation by an airline, the winning team would have their trip to nationals paid for. My jaw dropped.

"Seriously?" Minju asked. I could tell she had a sudden appreciation for book-related activities.

I wanted to win so badly I could taste it. I looked at the other teams. All of them were as eager as we were to get to the finals. I had to be realistic. Two of my teammates had never competed before. They didn't know how intense it got. The one-minute timer felt like five seconds if you didn't know the answer. Plus, seeing the other teams scribbling their answers shook your confidence. Some kids couldn't handle the pressure. I'd seen competitors storm out, or leave in tears, which meant the whole team defaulted.

I thought of Grandpa's advice. *Take it one question at a time.*

I took a deep breath.

"Pencils ready!" The Quizineer said. There was some shuffling as a player on each team picked up a pencil. "We begin! Round one, question one…"

CHAPTER 54

Tyson

Whatever Tyson had been expecting, it wasn't this. Some of his games in *Mutant-Z* were stressful, but the Kid Lit Quiz was ten times worse. The room was silent whenever the Quizineer asked a question, and then it erupted into whispers as each team discussed the answer.

Tyson couldn't help glancing over at Whyte Ridge. They always seemed to be finished first. The team would sit back with smug looks on their faces while everyone else hurried to write something down. After each round, the answer sheets were collected and judges corrected them, tallying up the totals. No one would know which three teams were going to the finals until all ten rounds were finished.

"I don't know half of these!" Minju whispered to Tyson.

But Emily and Jane did. A lot of times, it was just the two of them debating which answer to write down. Tyson had helped a few times. There'd been another question about his favorite childhood book, *Where the Wild Things Are*, and also one about *Wonder*. But as the rounds got more challenging, he'd basically sat back and let Jane and Emily handle things.

"Round five, question ten," the Quizineer said. "Death narrates this book."

Minju's face lit up. "I know the answer," she said, and wrote *The Book Thief.*

"Are you sure?" Emily asked.

"She's right," Jane said, meeting Tyson's eyes. "I read it too."

"Please turn in your papers to the judges. There will be a ten-minute break before the next round." Minju went to chat with someone she knew from basketball and Emily went to use the restroom, which left Tyson and Jane alone at the table.

There was a moment of awkwardness. They looked at each other, then burst out laughing. "I can't believe I didn't know it was you! When did you figure out I was X?"

A guilty flush rose up Tyson's neck. "It wasn't hard," Tyson said, choosing his words carefully. "You spend more time in the library than anyone else."

Jane frowned, thinking. "In your first note, you said you loved to read. Was that true?"

Tyson shook his head. "I thought if you knew the truth you wouldn't write back. Pretending to be someone who loved books seemed 'safer'."

Jane rolled her eyes at his pun, but then got serious. "So, you answered the note as a joke?"

Tyson mouth went dry. He didn't want to admit the truth.

But Jane's face broke into a grin. "Well, the joke's on you because look where you ended up—at Book Nerd Central."

Tyson made a pretend horrified face and looked around as if he'd just realized where he was. "Oh my god. You're right!"

Jane laughed. "And you must have got your marks up, or Mr. Morangi wouldn't have let you compete."

Tyson told her what the last week had been like, including the help he'd got from his friends, and then asked, "How's your grandpa?"

"He's going to be okay. The doctors said he might be home early next week. It was scary though. We didn't know if he was going to make it." They were both quiet until Jane spoke again. "It was Sienna who left the first note, you know. The Undercover Book Club was her way of helping me find a friend." Her eyes got a little watery when she said, "I can't wait to tell her it worked."

CHAPTER 55

Jane

There was another break between the last round and the finals. It was thirty minutes and allowed the judges to double-check the scores. Families who could make it, including mine, arrived to watch. Another man and woman walked in and waved at Tyson. "Are those your parents?" I asked. Tyson nodded sheepishly.

"I told them not to come but—"

"They're proud of you. Your mom only said it like ten times on the way over," Minju said.

The Quizineer took the stage and we all scurried back to our seats. He was going to announce who would be competing for the regional title. Had our team answered enough questions correctly?

"The team with the highest score is"—he looked out at the audience—"our reigning regional champions, Whyte Ridge Middle School!"

I gritted my teeth as they clapped and cheered for themselves.

"In second place…Langside Prep Academy!" A private school. The kids sat up straight, smiling and waving.

I squeezed my eyes shut. *Please. Please, let it be us.*

Even though I knew I had to be realistic, I'd already envisioned what would happen if we won. First, I'd call Sienna to tell her the good news, then, I'd take the trophy to the hospital and set it down on Grandpa's nightstand.

I didn't just want the win for myself, either. Minju, Emily and Hilman had shown they were real team players. So had Ms. Krauss by taking a day off to be with us. But mostly, I wanted the win for Tyson.

"Our third place team is"—everyone in the whole room held their breath—"Ecole Charleswood School!" Surprised giggles erupted from a table of girls.

"We didn't place." Tears of disappointment welled in my eyes. I looked at Tyson. He was staring at the Quizineer in disbelief. We'd come so far, I hated that it was over. How was I going to tell Sienna?

"*And*," the Quizineer said, "*tied* for third is Forest Hills!"

I gaped at the Quizineer. From the stands, Mom, Dad, and Kate cheered. So did Tyson's parents. Ms. Krauss beamed. Hilman gave a fist pump and shouted, "Yes!"

"That's right! We have four teams going to the finals." Tyson, Minju, Emily and I looked at each other. Even Emily burst into laughter at the news. We were going to the final round!

The stage had been set up with four long tables. There were chairs facing the audience, and a buzzer in front for each competitor. My hands were damp with sweat. "I feel like I'm gonna throw up," Tyson whispered. "Is that normal?"

"Yes." I nodded. It didn't help that the Whyte Ridge team had taken their spots and were literally flexing their intellectual muscles by firing off the names of the Newbery Award winners in chronological order.

"I might pee my pants," Minju said.

The Quizineer held his hand up and the crowd quieted. He reviewed the rules for the final round. If a team got an answer wrong, they couldn't answer again. All the teams started with ten points. A wrong answer deducted ten points, a correct answer won ten points. The first team to reach fifty points was the winner.

"The theme for today's final round is 'Name-the-Author.'"

I shared an excited grin with Tyson. "And now," the Quizineer began with a flourish, "the first question. This science fiction writer"—beside me Emily listened intently; this was her category—"was the daughter of a mathematician and a biologist. Born in 1925 in Liverpool, England, she went on to serve as a code breaker during the Second World War—"

The Whyte Ridge team buzzed. "Madeleine L'Engle."

"That is…incorrect!"

This could be our chance to pull ahead. The Quizineer continued as the Whyte Ridge team slumped in their seats, disqualified for the rest of this round. "She was almost fifty when her first book was published, but is best known for her Isis Trilogy—"

The buzzer on our table lit up. Emily leaned forward. "Monica Hughes."

"Correct!"

The other two teams muttered to themselves, shaking their heads. We were up by ten.

"Next question. This author, raised in Wales, was

of Norwegian descent." My finger hovered over the button. I was pretty sure it was Roald Dahl, but needed one more clue. "His many books for children are often told from the point of view of the child and feature adult villains who hate and mistreat children—"

I pressed my button, but it was Langside Prep's buzzer that lit up. The Quizineer pointed to their table. "Roald Dahl!"

"Correct!"

Our whole team groaned. The next few questions won points for Langside, Whyte Ridge and us. Ecole Charleswood School was trailing, but with a few wrong guesses by other teams, they could catch up.

"The score is twenty points for Charleswood, thirty points for Whyte Ridge, forty for both Langside Prep and Forest Hills." Tension in the room was thick. We could win if we got the next question right. I wiped my hands on my jeans and focused, my eyes glued to the Quizineer's mouth.

"This author lives and sets her books in New York City. Inspired by Madeleine L'Engle and E. L. Konigsberg, her characters often solve puzzles and mysteries, like Safer in—"

I pressed my button. I knew the answer. He was talking about *Liar & Spy*! My favorite book. "The author is—" My voice reverberated in the room as my mind went blank. I knew the title. I could see the cover. But the author…the name had vaporized in my brain. I stared, speechless, at the Quizineer. "Your answer," the Quizineer prompted.

"Rebecca Stead."

Tyson's voice rang loud and clear.

"Correct!" The Quizineer bellowed. "The winning team for the Super Book Invitational and this year's regional Kid Lit Quiz champions: Forest Hills School!"

Our team jumped up to cheer. In the audience Ms. Krauss hugged the coach next to her. Hilman was racing toward us and climbing the stairs to the stage. "We won!" Minju shouted.

I looked at Tyson. His face was still frozen in shock. "I can't believe it," he whispered.

"We're going to the nationals!" I told him. "Believe that!"

CHAPTER 56

Tyson

The news still hadn't sunk in at dinner as Tyson relived the whole competition for Ava and Max. He was glad his parents had seen it because they probably wouldn't have believed it otherwise.

"And now you get to go to nationals?" Ava asked.

"Lucky," Max said. It was the first time Tyson remembered his brother being jealous of him.

"It wasn't luck. It was skill," Tyson's dad said, clapping a hand on Tyson's shoulder. "Tyson stayed calm and collected under pressure."

Tyson's mom smiled and shook her head. "I thought your team was done for when Jane didn't know the answer."

Those few seconds of dead silence had felt like an hour. It still amazed Tyson that of all the authors the Quizineer could have picked, it had been one of the few that he knew.

So maybe it was a bit of luck.

That night, when Tyson lay in bed, he thought about the changes he'd gone through in the last month. A lot of them were thanks to Jane. Reading, for example, and pulling up his marks.

Could he keep them up? He had to if he wanted to go to nationals.

As a prize for the win, he'd left the Kid Lit Quiz tournament with a stack of books. They sat on his desk under the plaque that read *Kid Lit Quiz Regional Champion*.

Word spread quickly about the Forest Hills Kid Lit Quiz team's big win. A newspaper reporter came by to take photos and interview the team. "What was the winning ingredient for your team?"

"Determination," said Jane. She looked at Tyson. "And not giving up."

"I heard that you had some last-minute obstacles to overcome. A teammate moved away and your coach fell ill?"

Jane nodded. "My grandpa was the coach. He had a stroke. He's going to be okay, but our principal stepped in and then our coach from last year, Ms. Krauss, came to the rescue."

Tyson looked at the people in the room. Mr. Lee and Ms. Gill were there; Hilman, Emily, Jane, and Minju, who had decided to join the team permanently since Stefan had officially quit. Mr. Morangi and Mrs. Chin were at the back of the room too.

The reporter asked them to stand together so he could take a photo. "Here," Jane said, and handed Tyson the golden cup. "You should hold it. You answered the winning question." Tyson thought of the word he'd chosen that morning for the Other Words for Me bulletin board. It was May 1 and, just like every other month, Mr. Lee had passed out index cards.

This time, Tyson hadn't chosen a word to make kids laugh. He'd picked one that mattered. One that showed who he really was, and who he wanted to be. It was stapled in the middle of the board for everyone to see. Tyson thought of it as the reporter held up his camera. "Ready? 3-2-1."

"Champions!" the kids said in unison. Tyson's smile glowed as brightly as the trophy in his hands.

CHAPTER 57

Jane

"Are you sure you're up for this, Grandpa?" I asked. I'd met him at the front doors of Forest Hills School and we were walking toward the library. Dr. Sharma had given Grandpa permission to go about some of his daily routines. Which included coaching the Kid Lit Quiz team. He did look a lot better, even if he had to use a cane because he was still weak.

"I've been sitting around on my rear for too long. About time I got up and did something useful." The team was waiting for him in the library. We'd been practicing as best we could without Grandpa. But we'd all missed having a real coach.

On our way to the library, we passed a poster I'd

hung up to advertise a new club Tyson and I had created—The Undercover Book Club. Once a week, kids would meet to talk about what we were reading. We'd started a blog with our recommendations that was put on the school website. Mrs. Chin was letting us help her decide which books to buy for the library. It was book-nerd heaven.

And the Undercover Book Club wasn't just at Forest Hills. Sienna had started one too—with the help of her new book buddy, a girl named Alissa. They hadn't waited to meet like Tyson and me. Within a week of Alissa finding Sienna's note, they'd started hanging out after school. I'd get to meet Alissa at nationals and couldn't wait. I had a calendar in my room to count down the days.

I opened the door for Grandpa so he could walk into the library. "Why are the lights off?" he asked. As soon as he said those words, I flicked them on and Tyson, Emily, Minju, Hilman and Kate, jumped out from behind the bookshelves and shouted, "Surprise!"

Emily and I had made a *Welcome Back* banner. Welcoming someone, instead of saying goodbye, was a nice change.

Speaking of changes, Dad had put in his official request for retirement and it had been approved. After this posting, he'd become a civilian. Or as he said, a full-time dad. As much as Mom joked about how weird it would be to have Dad at home, we all felt better knowing we'd be together.

"What's all this for?" Grandpa asked looking around.

"For our favorite coach," Tyson said. Hilman held out a tray of cookies his mom had baked. *Gluten-free* cookies. It turned out his nervous stomach was actually a gluten sensitivity. Now that he knew what not to eat, his tummy troubles were over.

Grandpa waved away the praise. "You didn't have to go to all this trouble."

"We didn't have to. We wanted to," I said.

Grandpa put his arm around my shoulders. "We have three weeks to get ready for nationals!"

There was an audible gasp. *Three weeks!* Would we be ready? Tyson rubbed his hands together. "Let's get started!"

When practice was finished, we spent some time looking for new books to take out. Without realizing it, I wandered over to the *S* section and was standing right in front of *Liar & Spy*. It had been a while since I'd checked it. I'd assumed we'd stopped leaving notes for each other now that our identities had been revealed, but I opened the book, just in case.

Sure enough, there was a note tucked between the pages.

Dear Jane,
I'm not sure when you'll find this note. I'm writing it in the library. The reporter who interviewed us about winning regionals just left.

While he was taking our photo I realized you were the one who made it all happen. The only reason there was a team was because you didn't give up. Not on the team and not on me either.

I'm not going to say that books saved my life, but they did make it a lot better. Thanks for seeing me for who I am. And who I wanted to be, even if I didn't know it.

Sincerely,

Y

I folded the note and put it in my pocket. Then, *Liar & Spy* went back on the shelf.

Where it belonged.

The Undercover
Book List:

Liar & Spy by Rebecca Stead (Penguin Random House, 2012)

Harbor Me by Jacqueline Woodson (Nancy Paulsen Books, 2018)

Holes by Louis Sachar (Scholastic, 2000)

Wonder by RJ Palacio (Knopf, 2012)

The Book Thief by Markus Zusak (Alfred A. Knopf, 2006)

Hello, Universe by Erin Entrada Kelly (Harper Collins, 2017)

Bloom by Kenneth Oppel (Harper Collins, 2020)

Amari and the Night Brothers by B.B. Alston (Balzer + Bray, 2021)

The Barren Grounds by David A. Robertson (Puffin Books, 2020)

When You Reach Me by Rebecca Stead (Wendy Lamb Books, 2009)

Also mentioned in this novel:

Crossover by Kwame Alexander

City Spies by James Ponti

Front Desk by Kelly Yang

The Parker Inheritance by Varian Johnson

Where the Mountain Meets the Moon by Grace Lin

Harry Potter and the Sorcerer's Stone: Illustrated Edition by J.K. Rowling

Books by Susin Nielsen

Acknowledgments

There are always so many people to thank because books are like children and it takes the input of many people to raise them right! The team at Pajama Press has once again worked their magic. Thank you to Gail Winskill for being such a wonderful mentor and friend. WWGD (What Would Gail Do?) is the mantra by which I attack all things writing-related. More gratitude goes to Erin Alladin who, among many other things, writes the best cover copy an author could ask for; to Catherine Mitchell for her never-ending enthusiasm and marketing skills; to editor Chandra Wohleber for making the book better in all kinds of ways; to Lorena González Guillén for design and layout; and to Hayley Chrisp for her sharp-eyed proofing and keeping things running smoothly. A huge, heartfelt thank-you to Scot Ritchie for the artwork on the cover. It is perfection.

Selecting the books that would become part of the Undercover Book List was tricky. I have so many favorites! But this isn't *my* list—it belongs to Jane and Tyson. If you'd like to know which books I would suggest, please check out my website at www.colleennelsonauthor.com. It's updated often!

The Kid Lit Quiz is a real thing! Its name is actually the Kids Lit Quiz. If you'd like more information about this international competition, go to http://kidslitquiz.ca or https://www.kidslitquiz.com/usa.php

Thank you to Sheldon, James, and Thomas, and my frequent writing companion, Rosie.

An author and junior high school teacher, **Colleen Nelson** earned her Bachelor of Education from the University of Manitoba in her hometown of Winnipeg. Her previous works include the award-winning *Harvey Comes Home* and *Harvey Holds His Own*, which is a finalist for the 2020 Governor General's Literary Awards. *Sadia* won the 2019 Ruth and Sylvia Schwartz Award, and *Blood Brothers* was selected as the 2018 McNally Robinson Book of the Year for Young People. Her first picture book, *Teaching Mrs. Muddle*, was published in 2020. Colleen writes daily in between appearances at hockey rinks and soccer fields in support of her two sports-loving sons. The family's West Highland Terrier Rosie adds an extra-loveable dose of liveliness, squirrel-chasing, and shoe-chewing to their lives.

Don't miss Colleen Nelson's award-winning titles in

The Harvey Stories

- Book for Young People (Older Category)
- Winner of the Northern Lights Book Award
- Finalist for the Hackmatack Children's Choice Book Award
- Finalist for the Forest of Reading Silver Birch Fiction Award
- Finalist for the Rocky Mountain Book Award
- Finalist for the SYRCA Diamond Willow Award
- Bank Street Best Book

★ "Heartwarming and inspirational; a first purchase."—*School Library Journal* ★ *Starred Review*

"Much more than a lost-dog story."—*Kirkus Reviews*

"Dog lovers will drool over this multi-generational story."—*Booklist*

- Finalist for the Governor General's Literary Award
- Winner of the Northern Lights Book Award
- The Canadian Children's Book Centre Best Book for Junior & Intermediate Fiction

"A warmhearted tale of growth and connection."—*School Library Journal*

"Eminently believable. Characters...are lovingly developed."—*Kirkus Reviews*

"A charming novel...bettered by the love of a good dog."—*Foreword Reviews*

"Both *Harvey Comes Home* and *Harvey Holds His Own* are heartwarming tales that will be much loved by anyone who has ever owned a dog or wanted one."—*Canadian Children's Book News*

October -- 2021